"You're heaven, Maggie."

The whisper of his breath across her cheek gave Maggie sustenance. When she felt his mouth on her temple in a kiss, she sighed.

"I'm so glad you're here with me, Wes. I wouldn't know what to do without you...."

The quaver in her voice tore at him. He smiled against her temple; the strands of her hair felt silky beneath his lips. "Yes, you would, Red. You're strong and self-reliant."

"Not right now," Maggie whispered, and raised her chin to meet his hooded stare. Everything had been numb within her until just a few hours ago, but now she was beginning to feel again. Wes's smoldering blue eyes made her heart take wing, and she felt an incredible desire to kiss him. She needed Wes. She needed what he was silently offering her in the form of his embrace and what she saw so clearly written in his eyes....

Dear Reader,

Welcome to **Silhouette Special Edition** . . . welcome to romance. Each month, **Silhouette Special Edition** publishes six novels with you in mind—stories of love and life, tales that you can identify with—romance with that little "something special" added in.

And this month, we have a star-spangled surprise for you. To help celebrate the Fourth of July, we have two books that are dedicated to the Navy—and our country's valiant armed services. *Under Fire* by Lindsay McKenna is part of the thrilling WOMEN OF GLORY series—the hero and heroine are both naval pilots. *Navy Woman* by Debbie Macomber is set at a naval submarine base in the state of Washington—the hero is the commander of a vast fleet, and the heroine is a busy naval attorney. Three cheers for the red, white and blue—and the Navy! We're protected in the air as well as by sea! Happy Fourth of July.

Rounding out July are books by Ada Steward, Laura Leone and Carole Halston. And, as an added bonus, July brings the initial story of the compelling series SONNY'S GIRLS—*All Those Years Ago*, by Emilie Richards. The next installments in SONNY'S GIRLS due out in August and September, respectively, are *Don't Look Back* by Celeste Hamilton and *Longer Than . . .* by Erica Spindler. Don't miss these poignant tales!

In each **Silhouette Special Edition**, we're dedicated to bringing you the romances that you dream about—the type of stories that delight as well as bring a tear to the eye. And that's what **Silhouette Special Edition** is all about— special books by special authors for special readers!

I hope you enjoy this book and all of the stories to come.

Sincerely,

Tara Gavin
Senior Editor

LINDSAY McKENNA
Under Fire

Silhouette Special Edition

Published by Silhouette Books New York

America's Publisher of Contemporary Romance

To Leslie Kazanjian—
editor, mentor and most of all, friend.
I'll miss you. You're one of the best.

SILHOUETTE BOOKS
300 East 42nd St., New York, N.Y. 10017

UNDER FIRE

ISBN: 0-373-09679-8

First Silhouette Books printing July 1991

Printed in the U.S.A.

Books by Lindsay McKenna

LINDSAY McKENNA

spent three years serving her country as a meteorologist in the U.S. Navy, so much of her knowledge about the military people and practices featured in her novels comes from direct experience. In addition, she spends a great deal of time researching each book, whether it be at the Pentagon or at military bases, extensively interviewing key personnel. She views the military as her second family and hopes that her novels will help dispel the "unfeeling-machine" image that haunts it, allowing readers glimpses of the flesh-and-blood people who comprise the services.

Lindsay is also a pilot. She and her husband of fifteen years, both avid rock hounds and hikers, live in Ohio.

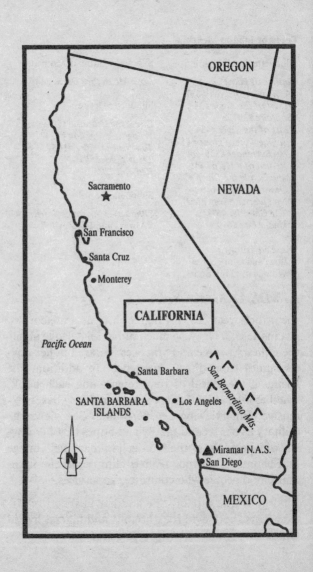

Chapter One

"**I** wouldn't fly with you again if you paid me to!"

Maggie Donovan glared at her radar information officer, Lieutenant Brad Hall. They stood tensely, inches apart, on the revetment area next to her F-14 Tomcat fighter jet. "Yeah? Well, you don't see me digging into my pockets to give you any money to do it, do you, Hall?"

Hall jabbed a finger in her direction. "You've got a real problem, Donovan. It's called 'You wanna run the whole goddamn show'!"

Her eyes narrowed in fury. "I'm the pilot! You're damn right I run the show. If anything happens to that bird, it's *my* responsibility and *my* rear on the line—not yours! You sit in the back cockpit and fiddle with your knobs and dials. You *should* do as I tell you. That's your job, mister, in case you forgot it.''

"Man, you're as tough as they come, Donovan," he rattled, taking a step back from her. "There's no way in hell I'm sitting in the cockpit with you again. I'm going to Commander Parkinson to ask for a transfer. Get some other poor jerk to listen to your tirades. I already feel sorry for whoever it is. You're worse than a nagging wife!"

Maggie, dressed in her flight suit and the body-hugging G-suit, jerked off her Nomex gloves and stuffed them into her pocket. "Hall, you can take a long walk off a plank, for all I care! I'll be going to Commander Parkinson, too. I'll make sure he gets the full story on your screw-ups in the cockpit."

"I didn't screw up. I'm just tired of you telling me how to do my job! No RIO in his right mind will fly with you. I've had it. Screw Red Flag and screw you!" Hall whirled on his heel and stalked off across the concrete apron, heading toward the waiting van that would take them back to Operations.

Breathing hard, Maggie tried to get control of her hair-trigger temper. "Good riddance," she whispered under her breath as Hall disappeared into the van. She waved at the driver, indicating he should go on without her. She needed time to calm down.

Day had just dawned over Naval Air Station Miramar, just north of San Diego, California. At 0800 the July sun's long rays shot westward toward the Pacific Ocean, not far from the station. Muttering under her breath, Maggie returned to her fighter and climbed up the ladder to retrieve her knee board.

"What a rotten start to the day." She rummaged around on the side of her ejection seat and located the board. Below, Maggie heard her crew chief's voice.

"Lieutenant Donovan, how did Cat perform this morning for you?"

"A hell of a lot better than my RIO did," Maggie retorted. She struggled to put her anger away. "Cat" was the name she had given her fighter. To many pilots a fighter was nothing but metal, wire and computers. But to Maggie, the F-14 seemed to come alive under her hands. And she'd given it a name worthy of its abilities.

Petty Officer First Class Chantal Percival, Maggie's dark-haired, darked-eyed crew chief, stood expectantly down below, dressed in a green one-piece uniform. Despite her petite size, Chantal, in Maggie's opinion, was the best crew chief in Fightertown, U.S.A. She had a magic touch with aircraft, and Maggie was glad Chantal was her mechanic for the daily flights. Besides, Maggie believed in women helping women, and she'd lobbied hard to get Chantal two years ago when she was first assigned to fly at Miramar. That was what the Sisterhood was all about, and Maggie enjoyed putting it into action every chance she got, working on behalf of enlisted women as well as the female officers based at the station.

Maggie climbed down the ladder. "Cat's back on target. You did good work on that heads-up display. Thank you." Crew chiefs were the backbone of any fighter squadron, and any good pilot knew it. Maggie's full name was printed on the side of the cockpit of her F-14, and just below her name was Chantal's.

Rapport between pilot and crew chief was critical, and those who cared for the aircraft had just as much pride in it as the pilot who flew it.

Chantal frowned. "I was just coming out of the hangar when I heard voices. Everything okay?" Her hair was cut very short. Absently, she pushed aside her wispy front bangs with grease-stained but capable fingers.

Maggie crouched down, unzipped her duffel bag and placed the knee board in it. At twenty-five, Maggie's own age, Chantal had been in the Navy seven years—she knew the wisdom of tiptoeing diplomatically around such touchy subjects as two officers having a verbal fight in public. As an officer, Maggie couldn't talk about the incident to an enlisted person. But, knowing Chantal, she'd heard every word Maggie and Hall had traded.

"Lieutenant Hall and I were just talking about our flight." That was the truth.

Chantal smiled knowingly, rocking back on the heels of her black boots. "He must have been real excited about something, huh?"

Maggie straightened and grinned back. "You might say that."

"Any flight discrepancies to report?"

"A few minor things. I'll note them in my discrepancy log and get them to you before noon," Maggie promised. "I'll see you later."

Chantal came to attention and saluted her smartly. "Yes, ma'am."

Maggie returned the salute and headed toward the huge hangar with the name Fightertown, U.S.A.

painted across it. Miramar was the home to Top Gun, where fighter pilots were trained and challenged to become the very best combat-worthy pilots in the world. The smell of JP-4 aviation fuel, the whine of jet engines and roar of several FA-18 Hornet fighters taking off behind her on the airstrip, made up the world that Maggie loved with a fierceness she never apologized for.

Frowning, Maggie turned to her immediate problem. Three months ago her boss, Commander Howard Parkinson, had chosen four of his best fighter pilots and their RIOs to participate in Red Flag, the Air Force equivalent to the Navy's Top Gun. This time the Air Force was making Red Flag open to the four best fighter pilots from each of the four services. Whoever won the contest would show the world which service had the best combat-ready pilots—it would be the ultimate plum in the world of military aviation competition.

To Maggie's unparalleled delight, she and Lieutenant Dana Turcotte had been chosen as part of the Navy's team. Obviously Parkinson wasn't chauvinistic about women's capability to handle combat flying. Instead he supported them completely, believing that women had even better reflexive skills than most male pilots. But he didn't say that publicly; only privately to Maggie and Dana. They were guinea pigs, he told them. They had to show military in general, and Congress in particular, that women pilots had the ability to be excellent in combat, too. The pressure on the two friends, and especially on Maggie, was appalling.

"Well, this is really going to pop Parkinson's brass buttons," Maggie muttered, entering the hangar. Brad Hall was an arrogant son of a bitch at best, and had been chosen exclusively because of his skills. He'd been pulled off fleet duty in the Far East to become her RIO specifically in preparation for Red Flag. For three months they'd suffered with each other. But the personality conflict between them had taken its toll. Maggie had had enough, and it had come to an explosive head this morning. What was Parkinson going to think?

Hitching a ride with another van headed for Ops, Maggie scowled. She ran her hand along the thick braid of red hair that she had pinned to the nape of her neck. She had very long hair, almost to her waist, but military regulations dictated that it was allowed only to brush the collar of her uniform.

Maggie braided her hair each morning and put it into a chignon instead of cutting it short as most women in the military finally did. The world she lived in was such a masculine one she insisted on remaining feminine. Her nails were always manicured and polished. Although she had never worn much makeup, she did wear lipstick regardless of whether she was flying or on the ground that day. Although the flight suits she wore were made for men, not women, Maggie had long ago started having them retailored to fit her tall form.

Her duffel bag contained many feminine articles. Once on the ground after a flight, she put on a tasteful pair of pearl earrings surrounded in gold. She also reapplied her lipstick and used a small spray bottle of perfume to neutralize some of the more unsavory fuel odors that inevitably lingered from around the hangars of the air station.

As she walked down the main hall of Ops after dropping her flight gear off at the women's locker room, Maggie wondered what Hall had told her boss. Knowing Hall, he'd probably exaggerated to make her look like the heavy. Would Parkinson remove her from Red Flag training and replace her with another pilot and RIO team?

Maggie broke out in a sweat at that thought. She slowed her step as she walked into the outer office of her boss. Yeoman Susan Walter, a woman in her early thirties, smiled.

"Your fame has preceded you, Lieutenant," she warned lightly.

Maggie grimaced. "I was afraid of that. Is the commander in?"

"Oh, yes. And he's been waiting for you."

"I'll bet. Thanks, Susan."

"Go right in."

The look on Susan's face told Maggie everything. Obviously Hall had come busting in here like a tornado. How much damage control would she have to implement to salvage her Red Flag training? Like those of all navy pilots, Maggie's hand shook. It was a natural result of landing on carrier decks, one of the most dangerous of all flight maneuvers. Maggie reached out and gripped the brass doorknob that led to Parkinson's office as Susan announced her over the intercom.

Maggie stowed her feelings deep inside as she entered the spacious office. Parkinson, in his early forties and partially balding, looked up. His wire-rimmed glasses sat on the bulbous end of his nose. He was a big man, appearing more so in a uniform that always seemed one size too small for him. Maggie quietly shut the door and came to attention in front of his desk.

"At ease, Maggie. Sit down, sit down." He gestured for her to take the chair nearest his maple desk.

"Thank you, sir." Her stomach quivered and knotted. Parkinson's dark brown eyes could rip someone apart if he chose. But Maggie knew that he liked having women in the service, and was at the forefront of getting them combat qualified in combat aircraft as part of the congressional trial. Maggie couldn't afford to have her career smeared by Hall. If she failed, then all the women who were struggling to follow in her footsteps would suffer because of it. Maggie couldn't live with that possibility. She sat up straight and alert.

"Brad Hall was in here," Parkinson said, leaning back in his leather chair and studying her.

"Yes, sir. I'm sure he was."

"He wasn't very happy, Maggie."

"I wasn't, either, sir."

"Want to tell me about it?"

Maggie didn't like the probing look Howard gave her. Had he swallowed Hall's tirade? His lies? Sweat popped out on her upper lip. To rant and rave immaturely about Hall would put her in a bad light with her boss. Diplomacy wasn't Maggie's forte, either, but she had to try to dredge some up from somewhere. Her career could be hanging on the line. Her fierce belief that a woman could do anything a man could might be scuttled by one lousy, jealous man.

"Sir, Lieutenant Hall and I have tried to adjust to each other over the last three months. We've had a personality conflict since the get-go."

"He called you a bitch."

Maggie's mouth tightened. "I suppose I can be that upon occasion, sir. It's been my experience, however, that if a woman is assertive, she's labeled a bitch, while if a man uses the same tactics, he's called bold and his aggressiveness is applauded."

Howard grunted. "He said you were a nagger."

"'Worse than a wife,' I believe, were his exact words."

"Yes. That, too. He accused you of telling him what to do all the time in the cockpit."

Squirming in her seat, Maggie controlled her temper with difficulty. Between clenched teeth, she said, "Sir, when I've got a bogey on my screen with the radar screaming in my ear that I've got him dead to rights and my RIO is sitting on his thumbs back there, I'm taking the shot with or without his help."

Parkinson's straight black brows rose slightly. "Did you get the kill this morning?"

"Yes, sir, I did."

"Good." He leaned forward. "Hall is refusing to fly with you again, Maggie, even if it means a court-martial. Those are pretty strong words for a career officer. He's serious."

"Yes, sir, I know he is."

Tapping his fingers on the files beneath his hand, Howard rolled his eyes. "I've got a dilemma, Maggie. Hall was chosen because he's the very best RIO the Navy has. In my opinion, you're our best combat pilot. I wanted the best paired with the best. We've only got three more months to prepare for Red Flag. You know how important teamwork and timing between the pilot and RIO is. It takes time to develop."

"No one realizes that more than I do, sir."

Getting up, he went to his coffee maker and poured himself a cup. "Want some?"

What Maggie wanted right now was a good, stiff belt of Irish whiskey. "No, thank you, sir."

"Cut the 'sir' stuff, Maggie. Relax. I'm not hauling your ass off this assignment, so stop looking like I'm going to end your career at any moment. Do you want some coffee?"

Relief cascaded through Maggie. She managed a slight smile. "Yes, sir... I mean, oh, hell. Yeah, give me a cup. My nerves are shot from squaring off with Hall."

Howard handed her a mug. He sat on the edge of the desk and thoughtfully sipped his coffee for several minutes before speaking.

"Why didn't you come to me sooner about him?" he asked finally.

Maggie got up, unable to sit still any longer. She'd always had an overload of nervous energy. "I thought it was me, at first."

"Oh?"

"You know how bullheaded and opinionated I can get."

"Yes. Like an overfocused laser on occasion."

Maggie nodded and sipped her steaming-hot coffee. "It's a weakness. But I also know my strengths, Commander. The first month with Hall was awful, but I assumed it was my fault. The second month, after changing tactics and trying my best to be diplomatic, nothing changed." She shrugged. "This last month I just said to hell with it and went back to being myself, hoping Hall would adjust."

"He didn't."

She sighed unhappily. "No."

"You're still buying into the double standard, Maggie."

She stared at Parkinson in disbelief.

"Close your mouth, Maggie. I didn't hit you, for heaven's sakes."

Snapping her mouth shut, she said, "Okay, what gives?"

"You followed the classic conditioned reflex of assuming it was *your* fault that Hall was reacting to you the way he did." The commander drilled her with a dark look. "Now, I know pilots and RIOs all have big egos, Maggie. They have to. Ego clashes are common in this little world of combat aviation. It takes a healthy ego to fly a thirty-five-million-dollar jet fighter on and off the heaving deck of a carrier. That RIO sitting behind you is helpless, dependent on your flight skills. He's not only got to think you're the best damn pilot in the world, but that he's the best damned RIO. Sometimes, seasoned RIOs get pretty plucky—even more egotistical than a pilot, if you can believe that. And when they do, they start encroaching on the pilot's territory. The problem usually only rears its head in combat circumstances.''

Maggie stood very still, assimilating Parkinson's statement. ''That's exactly what happened. Hall started second-guessing me when we were closing in for a kill on radar or the heads-up display. I wouldn't stand still for his badgering me to fire before I felt it was appropriate. We got into a lot of squabbles on the intercom.''

''I was hoping it wouldn't happen,'' Howard murmured, sitting down at his desk. ''But I knew there was a possibility it could.''

Her eyes rounded. ''Well, why didn't you warn me?''

''Maggie, if I told you everything I've learned, would you remember it, much less use it?''

''I'd give it one hell of a try.''

He shook his head. ''Making a good fighter pilot is part teaching and part letting them learn from their own experience. You've had three RIOs here at Miramar over the years. Hall was your fourth. You got along well with the first three. That's why I didn't swallow all of Hall's accusations. Unfortunately this assignment went to his head. Being touted as the best RIO in the Navy is no small boast, Maggie. He swallowed his own press—hook, line and sinker.''

She snorted. ''And I see my responsibility as the first woman fighter-pilot in the Navy to be just the opposite. It's a load to carry. If I screw up, every other woman will be pointed at and told she's just like me. And that's not true. Why didn't Hall see his assignment the way I do?''

"Because the double standard's still alive and kicking, Maggie. Hall's a man, and moving higher up on the ladder of success breeds ego, confidence and, in some, a swelled head. Because you're a woman, you took exactly the opposite tack: your elevated status equaled responsibility and nothing more. Women have had it drilled into them for five thousand years that they're to be meek and subservient."

Maggie sat back down, deep in thought. "Okay, so I've learned a valuable lesson, Commander. But this sure isn't going to help us at Red Flag. How can I train a new RIO to work with me when it's only three months away?"

Howard raised his brows. "Good tactical assessment of our problem."

Maggie felt a tiny bit better when Parkinson framed it as "our" problem and not just hers. She liked his ability to work as a team, guiding everyone toward working for a common goal.

"However," Parkinson went on, "I also want you to realize, Maggie, that Hall may have had some valid criticism of your performance. I'm not talking about his name-calling."

Her conscience pricked her. "Yes, sir, I do tend to come down on the RIO when things get tense. I just don't want to get nailed by the enemy, that's all. I *have* to perform outstandingly every time."

"I know that, Maggie, and that's why I'm not hauling you on the carpet over Hall's transfer. The work between a pilot and an RIO is like a marriage. It can be made in heaven or hell."

Quirking her mouth, Maggie nodded. "Well, ours went straight to hell," she conceded softly. "I know I didn't help things, sometimes. But, dammit, Hall just got my goat!"

"No, he pushed the buttons on that temper of yours."

"I've been working on corralling it. Honest to God, I have."

"Hmm." Parkinson eyed several folders on his desk. "I've got three new RIO candidates flying in today for Top Gun classes. I'm going to look over their records and see what we've got to choose from. Then, I'll pick one for you—"

"Sir, may I interview the potential candidate?" Maggie knew she shouldn't even ask such a question. In the military system, you took what you got without saying anything.

"That's a highly unusual request."

Maggie placed her hands flat on his desk, holding his gaze. "Yes, sir, it is. But I'm in a highly unusual situation."

"Don't use reverse female chauvinism on me, Maggie. It won't work."

"No, I didn't mean it that way!"

"Sure?"

Maggie felt some heat creep into her cheeks. She knew she was blushing. Brazenly, she held her boss's dead-level gaze. "Yes, sir."

"You're trying to bluff your way through this, Maggie." He grinned. "But, I don't blame you. Okay, I'll let you interview your new RIO."

"And if I don't think the chemistry's there after a familiarization flight?"

"You can check out the other two. Fair enough?"

A smile leaked from her tightly compressed lips. "More than fair, skipper. Thanks." She straightened into an at-attention posture.

"When I get done, which will probably be sometime tomorrow, I'll contact you over at the hangar and get you and the potential RIO together," Parkinson growled. "Now, get out of here, Donovan. I've got work to do."

Smiling, Maggie said, "Yes, sir!" then made a neat about-face and left his office.

Because she was part of the Top Gun instruction team at Miramar, her office was located in Ops on the second floor. Humming a lively Celtic tune under her breath, she felt the weight on her shoulders dissolve. Maybe Hall leaving halfway through the six months of Red Flag training would be okay, after all.

In her small, plain office, Maggie got down to work. Every once in a while, the thought of her new RIO leaked into her mind. Would she be able to get along with him? What would he be like? A good pilot-RIO combination was like a winning dance-competition couple: their every movement smoothly choreographed and flawlessly executed. A bad combo was like the result of a shy ten-year-old boy getting dragged out onto the dance floor by an overenthusiastic girl: a disaster in lack of coordination. But the combat dance a jet-fighter couple performed in the air was more critical than dance competition on the ground. The deadly dance they performed together in the sky could keep them alive . . . or let them die.

So, what would her partner be like? The professional who knew she had to be the boss in the air? Or the gawky ten-year-old boy stumbling over his own feet?

Chapter Two

"Hey, Lieutenant Donovan!" an air crewman from the side office in the hangar shouted. "Commander Parkinson wants to talk to you on the phone."

Maggie was head deep in one of Cat's engines with Chantal when the petty officer called to her. Muttering, Maggie carefully withdrew from the engine intake, with Chantal at her side. Her crew chief gave her a clean rag to wipe off her hands.

"Thanks, Chantal."

"Maybe news about your new RIO?" Chantal guessed.

Maggie glanced at the watch on her left wrist. It was exactly noon. "I hope so. I'll be back a little later."

"Yes, ma'am. Good hunting," the chief teased.

With a grin, Maggie settled her garrison cap on her head. "Thanks." She entered the little hangar office and picked up the receiver.

"I think—" Parkinson's voice on the phone held a degree of humor "—that you're going to like your replacement RIO, Maggie."

Her heart beat a little harder. Nerves. "Oh?"

"His name is Lieutenant Wes Bishop. I wanted you to come over and check him out here at Ops, but he said he'd rather meet you at the officers' club for lunch."

She frowned. "Great." Bishop must be one of those jocks who thought he could impress her with lunch and a bottle of wine.

"Don't jump to conclusions. He's a good candidate. Spend all the time you need with him, give him an FAM flight and then get back to me with your assessment and decision."

"Yes, sir." Maggie hung up the phone. Her dark green flight suit had smudges of grease and God knew what else on it from helping Chantal tinker with Cat's engine. With her degree in aeronautical engineering, Maggie knew a great deal more about the mechanical workings of her plane than most pilots.

"I look like a pig."

"Ma'am?" the petty officer behind the desk asked, raising his head from his paperwork.

"Oh...nothing." Maggie spread out her hands before her. Last night she'd taken the polish off her nails to let them breathe for a day or two before coating them with another color. Groaning, she realized that grease was stuck stubbornly beneath them. Great. She was going to look like a grease monkey to this guy.

Why do I care? He ought to be more worried about what I think of him. With that thought, Maggie tossed the rag into the receptacle for just such items, picked up her purse and slung it over her left shoulder. Leaving the hangar, she hitched a ride in a truck going in the direction of the O club.

On the way over, Maggie took the mirror out of her purse. Her hair looked frizzy. Not that she had curly hair, but a number of auburn strands had worked their way out of the chignon, especially from her temple area. Putting on some lipstick made her feel a bit better, but Maggie knew, at best, she looked more like a mechanic today than a pilot.

And then her temper got the better of her. *Why should I worry what I look like? Double Standard Donovan. Knock it off. This is business. Strictly business!*

Of course, Maggie thought as the truck dropped her off at the O club, she was going to check out Bishop with a fine-tooth comb. Her mother had trained her to pay attention to faces, voice tones, body language and eyes. Eyes were the most important consideration.

As she hurried up the concrete sidewalk, she prayed Bishop's eyes showed honesty and intelligence. Ignoring the small palm trees and bougainvillea that surrounded the spacious O club, Maggie entered through the double doors.

Taking off her cap, she hesitated in the foyer. Bar or dining room? She snorted softly. Bishop, she was sure, was probably in the bar—like every other macho Navy jet jock. She hated going there because the civilian women groupies were always hanging around trying to hook up with a flier. The games they played made her nauseous. Taking a deep breath, Maggie dived into the huge bar. It was crowded for this time of day, and a number of civilian women mingled with the men dressed in uniform and flight suits. The hunt was on.

How was she going to find Bishop? It meant she had to walk up and down the entire bar looking at the name on each man's flight uniform. The cigarette smoke and the loud hard-rock music jarred her frayed nerves, but Maggie persevered, eyeballing each man's name tag.

After fifteen minutes of close inspection, Maggie still hadn't found Bishop in the bar. Going back out to the foyer, she frowned. Okay, she was wrong about Bishop. He wasn't a groupie jock. At least, not today. Maybe he was on his best behavior. Who knew? She headed to the dining room, a much quieter, well-lit place with lots of greenery, soft music and a far better clientele, in her opinion.

At the door, she halted. Although the dining room was filled to capacity, Maggie had no trouble singling out her RIO. Her blood boiled. She saw Brad Hall leaning over another man in a dark green flight suit, talking intently. *Hall.* Maggie narrowed her eyes. The seated man had to be Bishop—she could barely make out his name in gold print emblazoned on the black leather patch on his flight uniform.

Was Hall a buddy of Bishop's? Maggie's hands turned damp as she considered the possibility. Clenching her garrison cap, she gave herself time to check out Bishop without being discovered. Hall was too deeply in conversation with his fellow RIO to even notice her presence.

When Hall moved from in front of Bishop, it gave Maggie her first clear view of him, and her first impression. Her heart thudded once in her breast to underscore her strictly feminine response to Bishop. God, but he was sinfully handsome! Bishop looked more like a movie star than an honest-to-God RIO earning a Navy paycheck.

Maggie had to jerk herself up short and stop reacting like that. He must be at least six foot four. He was a big man with broad shoulders, a square face and a strong jaw to go with it. Olive-skinned, Maggie observed, with short black hair and expressive brows above his intense blue eyes. She relaxed slightly. Good, Bishop's eyes were large and spaced far apart. His high cheekbones and eagle-like nose created a wonderful balance for those appealing eyes that seemed to dance with mischief. As her gaze drifted down to his mouth, Maggie felt herself go weak and shaky.

Stop this! Maggie Donovan, you're acting like a girl who's fallen in love with her first boy! Idiot! But she couldn't help it as she gazed at the lazy curve of Bishop's beautifully molded mouth. The lower lip was large and flat, and the corners turned up naturally, as if a slight smile hovered perpetually around his mouth. His upper lip was sculpted and slightly smaller. But together, Maggie decided, those lips composed the most attractive mouth she'd ever seen on any man in her life.

I'll bet he's a real heartbreaker with the groupies. Tall, dark and handsome. Women would fall all over this guy. Overall, Bishop was large boned: but his hands were well shaped, with long fingers—almost artistic, in Maggie's estimation. He looked Italian, but her finely honed instincts didn't completely agree with that judgement. There was a certain aura of danger about Bishop—something that made her feel abnormally unsure of herself.

When he smiled at something Hall said, Maggie groaned inwardly. Bishop's face beamed; his dazzling smile made her heart race. But his eyes remained cool. Bishop didn't really think whatever Hall had said was humorous; his eyes would have reflected it. Maggie frowned. No doubt Hall was filling Bishop's ear about her. Damn it! She didn't need to get off on the wrong foot with him. As she started forward, Maggie knew it was a two-way street: Bishop could refuse this assignment with her, too. And if her boss felt this man was the best for the job, she didn't want to lose him because of Hall's criticism of her—justified or not.

"It's a small world," Maggie challenged Hall, coming up and halting a foot away from her ex-RIO.

Wes Bishop rested his chin against his hands, and watched with interest. Something had whispered to him earlier to look up toward the entrance of the dining room. He knew immediately that the red-haired woman in a green flight uniform had to be Maggie Donovan. Her five-minute inspection of him made him smile to himself. He'd pretended to pay full attention to Brad's story of woe but the whole time, his senses had been acutely focused on Maggie.

"What are you doing here, Donovan?" Hall growled, straightening and standing next to Bishop's chair.

"It's noon and it's time to eat. I have a stomach just like you do, Hall."

Wes winced. Man, she could come out firing when she wanted to. It was obvious she and Hall didn't like each other.

Brad glared at her. "I was just filling in my old friend, Wes Bishop, on working with you. I understand he's your new RIO."

Maggie glanced over at Wes, who was staring innocently up at her. That damned mouth of his was curved in an angelic shape, and she bridled. "If there's any filling-in to do, it's my responsibility to do it, Hall. Not yours. Now, if you'll excuse us, I've got to interview Lieutenant Bishop."

Hall shrugged. He patted the other RIO's shoulder. "Later, Wes."

"Yeah. Later, Brad. See you around."

Nervously, Maggie sat down opposite him. She stowed her purse and garrison cap beneath her chair. Offering her hand after Hall left, she said, "I'm Maggie Donovan. Commander Parkinson told me you'd be over here."

Wes noted how long and slender Maggie's hand was. She didn't have pretty model's hands; fingers were too large-knuckled. He clasped and shook it, appreciating her strong grip. "Wes Bishop. Nice to meet the world-famous lady combat-pilot."

With a grimace, Maggie noticed his firm yet gentle shake. He had wonderful hands, she thought. Trying to get her wildly rolling feelings under control, Maggie worked to contain her strictly feminine reaction to Bishop and get down to the business at hand. It was impossible to do.

"There's been too much publicity on me over the past couple of years," she griped. "None of it was fair, and the rest was mulch for those rags. I hope you didn't believe what you read."

Wes smiled and picked up his coffee cup, studying her over the rim. "I prefer meeting a person face-to-face before making up my mind." She was feminine despite her lanky frame, he decided—and touchingly vulnerable. Her hand shook as she picked up the glass of water and sipped. Partly from flying off carrier decks, he thought. Still, there was a softness to Maggie that appealed strongly to him. There was anxiety in the depths of her lovely emerald-green eyes. Automatically, Wes wanted to put her at ease.

"You're not what I expected, I have to admit."

Maggie tried to appear at ease, although she felt anything but. She tried to figure out her reaction to Wes Bishop logically. Sure, she was nervous about meeting him as an RIO; but more, her heart was doing wild leaps every time he rested those steady blue eyes on her. When had a man's looks ever made her feel like this? Maggie blamed her nerves. "Oh?"

"Yeah. I expected a hard-edged broad who walked with a macho swagger and tried to pretend she was one of the boys. You aren't."

Gawking at him for an instant, Maggie was nonplussed. "You shoot straight from the hip, don't you?"

"I see you didn't waste any words on Hall, either," Wes pointed out mildly.

"Touché," she admitted. The waitress came over and Maggie gave her order. She wasn't really hungry. This man made her so nervous she wanted to drink to quell her reaction, but she needed a clear head so she ordered coffee instead.

Placing her elbows on the table and resting her chin against her clasped hands, Maggie said, "Commander Parkinson sent me over here."

"I know. To check me out."

"It's for both our benefits."

"That's fine. I understand. Hall has a problem with you."

"Is that what he told you?"

"Don't get your hackles up, Lieutenant."

"I will if you swallow the hogwash he fed you."

Wes grinned and moved the dainty cup slowly around in its saucer, his large hand huge in comparison to the china. "You've got a very distrustful look in those pretty green eyes of yours," he baited.

"And you can cut through the jock talk, Bishop. This is strictly business between us." Still, she'd liked his low, rough tone when he'd complimented her.

"Just because I compliment you doesn't mean I'm after your body, Ms. Donovan." Not that it wasn't a pleasant thought. Wes liked her lean, greyhound grace. Maggie wasn't beautiful in the conventional sense. She had a long face to go with that long body of hers. Her eyes were like huge green emeralds framed with thick red lashes. Her nose, he was sure, had been broken, with a bump to attest to it. The rest of it flowed straight and clean down to fine, thin nostrils that flared when she was taking offense. Wes couldn't decide which he liked more about Maggie: her eyes that telegraphed every emotion, or that pursed set of full lips that had just a touch of impishness.

Maggie sat digesting his statement. "You give as good as you get, don't you, Bishop?" she said after a moment.

"I guess it comes with the territory, Donovan. Pilots think they run the show up there."

"RIOs think *they* run it."

Wes leaned forward, a lazy grin on his mouth. "The truth is, we run it together."

She felt a glimmer of hope. "You aren't just B.S.-ing me? You mean that?"

"To use the words of Commander Parkinson, pilots and RIOs are in a marriage of sorts." He looked her over nice and slow, deliberately testing her reaction. She frowned. "I wouldn't mind being 'married' to you. And I'm not such a bad catch, either."

Maggie stared hard at Wes. The woman in her entertained the fleeting thought of him as a husband. No, he wasn't a bad catch. And then Maggie bridled at her foolish thoughts. Where were they coming from, anyway? "Where'd you get your sense of humor?"

"The same place you got yours, Ms. Donovan. My mother's an Italian woman of fire and passion. My father's half Cherokee and half Irish." His grin widened. "I got my mother's skin color and hair. My father gave me the high cheekbones, blue eyes, his nose and mouth, not to mention my wonderful personality."

"Passion, huh?" She had to tear her gaze from the lazy smile that pulled at his mouth—a mouth that any woman would be crazy not to want to kiss.

"Nothing wrong with a little passion, is there?"

Maggie's eyes narrowed. Wes had her way off-balance. Normally she held her own with any arrogant jet jock. "Depends upon where the passion is emphasized, Bishop." Yes, he was a man of passion, there was no doubt, and Maggie went hot and shaky inside. Was she going crazy? Was the stress finally getting to her? Never had she reacted so strongly and immediately to a man. It had to be her imagination, the stress of her job.

"Oh." He gave her an innocent look. "Well, of course it would be a passion to be the best damn RIO you ever had while we work together in the cockpit to win Red Flag."

Maggie sat back and her laugh came out full and rolling. With a shake of her head, she rested her elbows on the table again. "You always say the right thing, Bishop?"

His eyes danced with merriment. He liked her full-throated laughter. He liked a woman who could laugh at herself, as well as at the world around her. "I can't blame my diplomacy on my Italian side because my mother has absolutely none."

"And the Irish have no capacity for diplomacy."

"That's true. I guess the Cherokee blood from my father gave me the saving grace of knowing when to say something and when to keep my mouth shut."

"I have a hard time believing any jet jock can keep his mouth shut."

"You're afraid I'll try to override your decisions in the cockpit?"

Serious now, Maggie said, "Yes, to be honest about it. Hall tried it, and I wouldn't stand for it."

"I like a woman who values truth above everything else."

Rolling her eyes, Maggie heard him chuckle at her reaction. It was a low, rumbling chuckle. There was absolutely nothing about Wes that rubbed her the wrong way. She was curious about him. No man had ever kept up with her lightning tongue the way he did.

"That wasn't a line."

"Sounded like one. I've heard that so many times in the bar over there, it's not even funny."

"Can't blame those boys for trying to hit on you," Wes told her congenially, sipping the coffee.

"'Boys'?" Maggie blurted, because she wondered if Wes really was drawn to her as much as she was to him on strictly a personal level. No, he couldn't be. Not ever. "And I suppose you're a man compared to them? Oh, brother."

"I'm twenty-nine—older than most of those youngsters in there hanging out at the bar with their arms around groupies. How old are you?"

His sudden seriousness rattled Maggie. "Twenty-five."

"At least you're out of diapers."

"I was walking at nine months. What about you?"

"A year."

"A little slow, aren't you, Bishop?"

"Slow start, strong finish. I'm very good at crunch time, Ms. Donovan."

In the cockpit, when they were searching for the "enemy" on radar, things could get very tense. Some RIOs got too excited and started yelling. That would upset a pilot who preferred a more laid-back, composed RIO. "I'm glad to hear that."

"So, this is supposed to be an interview of sorts," Wes said congenially, leaning forward, his elbows also on the table. "I have to size you up and vice versa. Parkinson feels we can work well together. He laid out the facts about this Red Flag assignment. It's only for three months, and after that, I'll be able to go back to my squadron out on the carrier. I consider this a three-month vacation."

"Of what? Working with a woman combat-pilot? Or Red Flag?"

"Both."

She probed him mercilessly. Somehow, Maggie *had* to get out of her emotional response to him and keep it strictly business. "Okay, I'm taking off the kid gloves with you, Bishop, because I don't have any time left to waste. I've got to find a damn good RIO who can train fast, take orders without a lot of back talk, and help us win Red Flag for the Navy. I don't like, nor do I tolerate, male chauvinist pigs. I believe a woman can do anything a man can—with some physical limitations, of course. When we're in the air working together, my sex doesn't enter into the equation, and yours doesn't, either. We're a team—not a man and woman working together. I've worked my butt off getting this far, and I carry more responsibility than I care to admit—for all women—as a result. I know I'm a symbol in this test Congress has seen fit to try out. If I screw up, I screw up for all women. A lot of combat pilots don't like me and think that when the chips are down I can't fly or fight just as well as they can."

She halted and watched him. Wes sat relaxed, with all his attention on her. If what she'd said didn't faze him, there was hope. Maggie saw no defensiveness or anger in his eyes. "I've been training Top Gun pilots here for almost two years. Out there over the desert in the restricted area where we fly, I'm the 'aggressor.' My whole reason for flying is to outwit, outfox and outmaneuver these hotshots and make them realize where they're weak in their flying skills so they can improve and become better combat pilots.

"On the ground at debrief, we go over every dog-fight sequence. Nine times out of ten, I win my confrontations in the air with these guys. They don't like it because they're getting beaten by a woman, and women aren't supposed to be able to fly half as well as they can. My stats can't be argued with, Bishop. That's why Commander Parkinson chose me to head up the Navy Red Flag team. I need an RIO who wants to win just as badly as I do. I'm competitive, but not with anyone but myself. I don't expect anything more of you than I do of myself. I'm not a screamer in the cockpit. I'd hope we can work smoothly in an adult way. I can't stand childish pouting or games being played when everything's on the line."

Wes sat there for a long moment, digesting Maggie's impassioned words. The waitress came and delivered her salad and his hamburger. He thanked her and worked at putting mustard and catsup on the burger. Maggie glanced up at him from time to time, running her fork disinterestedly around in the shrimp salad.

"I don't have a problem with what you said." Wes took a huge bite of his hamburger, watching Maggie's instantaneous reaction. Her eyes widened enormously, and he tucked his smile away. He knew she'd thought he would challenge her brass-knuckled delivery of her expectations. "Matter of fact," he added, picking up a french fry, "I totally agree with you."

Her nostrils flared and she pushed the salad aside, zeroing in on him. "Okay, what do you expect out of this?"

Her intensity pleased him. A damn good combat pilot had the ability to focus sharply on what was ahead of him—or her, in this case—blocking out everything else. "I kinda like the idea of working with a woman. Never have before, and that intrigues me."

Her heart banged violently against her ribs. Was he honestly drawn to her? No. Every other male she'd worked with over the years had been all business, regarding her not as a woman, but as a pilot—a genderless person who sat in the front seat flying the plane. Wes's hooded look in her direction unstrung Maggie. "Look, if you're talking—"

"Whoa, let me finish." He held up his hand. Then, teasingly, he asked, "Do you always interrupt people?"

Chastised, Maggie nodded. "Yeah, one of my bad habits. Go ahead."

"I like that: you can admit your faults."

"I didn't apologize, Bishop."

"I didn't expect you to. But most male pilots wouldn't have admitted anything, either."

"So?" Maggie challenged.

"So, I like your ability to be a human being, not a tin god in the cockpit like those boys think they are."

Her smile was rueful. Most fighter pilots were in their early or middle twenties. With Wes being an "old man" at twenty-nine, she imagined they did look like boys to him. "I like your maturity already."

"Good." He pushed the plate of french fries toward her. "Here, have some."

Wrinkling her nose, Maggie said, "No, thanks. They're pure grease."

"Wouldn't hurt you to put on a little weight, you know."

His personal comment shook her. Bishop had the unnerving ability to get her trust, and when she gave it to him, even something as innocent and caring as his observation about her lack of weight made her defensive. Maggie didn't have time to ask herself why she reacted so strongly.

"Let's stick to the conversation at hand," she told him. "What do you expect from me?"

"What I'm getting right now—your honesty and how you see things going down. I don't sit in the back seat with a jerk for a pilot, either. My life's in your hands. I don't have a second set of controls in case you screw up. All I can do is sit back there and pray you can get us out of trouble flight-wise."

"I've never lost a plane."

"Not even close?"

"No."

"You been in any flat spins?"

"Yeah."

"How many?"

Maggie knew flat spins were the most dangerous flight situation a plane could find itself in. Fifty percent of the time, the aircraft was lost because the pilot was unable to pull it out of the flat spin. She held Bishop's unrelenting gaze, liking his clear, crystalline blue eyes. "In training, six times. In combat practice, three times because jet-wash compression stalled my engines. I was lucky to be at high enough altitudes to pull it out and not have to eject."

Bishop nodded. "Truthful to a fault, aren't you? Not many pilots would tell me about those last three."

"Honesty is something I live my life by."

"Good," Wes praised. He was starting to really like Maggie Donovan.

"Look, I've had my trial by fire. I've had instructors who wanted to wash me out from the time I stepped foot into naval aviation. Not only did I learn how to fly, but I had to outfly them just to pass the course. I had to fly twenty times better than any male candidate." She held up her long, slim hands. "I've got 'hands,' Bishop. Flying's in my blood. I breathe, eat and sleep it. It's my life. I don't ever want anything other than what I've got now. I like where I'm at, and I like myself. I respect what I've got, and yes, I'm always pushing the envelope on myself."

"Nothing else interests you?" Wes asked suddenly, changing tactics.

"What else is there except flying?" Maggie asked in surprise, a defensive tone in her voice.

"I don't know," Wes murmured, chewing on another french fry. "How about a homelife? A husband? Maybe some kids down the line?"

She scowled.

"That wasn't a chauvinistic comment."

"Sounded like it."

"That's negative. So, what else interests you in life, Maggie Donovan?" Had she deliberately sidestepped her marital status? There was no wedding ring on her left hand, but pilots weren't allowed to wear jewelry when they flew, anyway. He smiled slightly when he saw her cheeks flush a bright pink. Despite her focus and assuredness about what she wanted out of life, Maggie still was very much a human being with obvious weaknesses and strengths. That made her endearing. His heart squeezed in his chest as he thought about reaching over and caressing that fiery cheek with his hand.

Shifting uncomfortably in her chair, Maggie shrugged. "I don't know." Part of her was pleased that he showed personal interest in her—at the same time, it was unsettling as hell.

"Come on, you can do better than that."

She crossed her arms over her breasts and studied her feet, which she shoved out beside the table. Her flight boots were like polished ebony mirrors. No, Wes was just good with people, Maggie decided. If she thought for a second that he was genuinely interested in her as a woman, she might have opened up on a more personal level.

With a sigh, Wes wiped his mouth with the white napkin. Maggie wasn't going to cooperate. Obviously she felt he was overstepping his bounds, putting them on a personal basis. Well, wasn't he? He ignored the question and the answer. "Tell me where you live."

"It's an apartment," Maggie said finally, and then added when he probed her with those blue eyes, "In a large complex."

"Large? Small?"

Petulantly, she shot him a glance. "I live over in Poway near my two friends, Molly and Dana. They're officers stationed here at Miramar with me. My apartment has two bedrooms and I transit from there, using it to sleep after flying."

"Any pets?"

"Of course not. How could I? I get over to Miramar at 0600 and usually don't leave until 2100."

"Whew! Those are long hours."

"When you're a woman, you've got to put that kind of time into your career."

"Why?"

"Because a woman can't make it in the military just being good. I have to stand out."

Wes couldn't disagree. "Bingo. So, you don't really have any life except flying."

"That's right. How about yourself?" Maggie jerked in a breath. What was she doing? Now *she* was getting personal and treading on thin ice. Still, he interested her as no other man ever had.

"I live over in Poway, too. Right now I'm renting an apartment at Flamingo Corners."

"Yeah, that's about two miles away from our apartment facility. I'm at Casa de la Madre Tierra."

"I've driven by it. Nice place."

"So, does your life revolve around flying?"

"Yes and no. When I'm home, I like it. When I'm stationed on a carrier or an air station, I like to fly. I don't know whether Commander Parkinson told you or not, but I'm recently divorced. My wife's remarried to a guy in Ohio. We have a little girl, Annie. She's five years old and the cutest thing you've ever seen." His voice grew soft with feeling. "I love Annie with my life." And then he looked over at her. "What about you?" He wanted to know if she was married or not. "Any family?"

A huge part of Maggie sagged in relief to find out Wes wasn't married. "I'm single, but my family lives in Sacramento, and we're close. I'm a first-generation American. My father and mother came over from Dublin, Ireland, forty-five years ago with very little money and a desire to live in America. Dad got a job as an Amtrak engineer, and he's still doing it to this day. My mom raised four Irish-hellion girls."

"You the oldest?"

"No, the youngest."

"Ah, the baby of the family."

She laughed. "It doesn't mean a thing, Bishop, so forget the psychological ramifications."

"I was firstborn and look at me: a natural leader, goal oriented and highly successful at what I do."

"Are you happy, though?"

Wes gave her a strange look. There was more than just flash to Maggie. "I like a balance to my life between job and home. No apologies that I like to sit down with a beer and watch a football game on TV while my wife makes me a great meal."

She rolled her eyes. "Sooner or later I knew that was coming."

"There is life after flying, you know."

"Not in my book. Not ever. This is it for me, Bishop, and you've got to appreciate where I'm coming from if you're going to work with me."

He drained the last of the coffee from the bottom of his cup and sat back. "Babies of the family are supposed to be sheltered and protected from life. They seek the easiest route and aren't goal oriented at all."

"Shoots down your theory, doesn't it?"

With a shrug, Wes said, "Maybe. Maybe not." Although Maggie was a stridently confident woman, and one of the few he'd ever met of that stripe, there was something that nagged at him. Beneath all her bravado, chutzpah and strength, he sensed there was a hidden source of softness that she kept well protected from him. Could he blame her? No. In the male military environment, a woman would get eaten alive if she didn't have proper defenses in place to survive the hardness of its demanding life-style. And from all appearances, Maggie was surviving and thriving beautifully in the environment. But at what cost to herself? he wondered.

"Look, I want to take this cross-examination of each other a step further. I want to take you up on a FAM flight and see how you do." She held his amused gaze. "And you can check me out, too. Let's see if we can get our act together up there and work as a team.

My wingwoman, Lieutenant Dana Turcotte, will be the aggressor and try to jump us. I've got permission from Commander Parkinson to set up this flight and dogfight. Are you game?''

Wes got to his feet and put enough money on the table for both meals. ''Let's boogie.''

Maggie nodded, liking his style. ''I'll pay for my own meal, Bishop. Thanks, anyway.''

''No, it's mine this time.''

''I pay my own way.''

He gave her a dazzling smile while reaching out and capturing her by the upper arm and gently guiding her through the dining room. ''I know you do. Next time, you can pay for my meal. Fair enough?''

That smile melted all her insistence. How could *any* woman ever resist his charm? Maggie wondered. She scowled. ''If there is a next time.''

Laughing, Wes dropped his hand from her arm as they reached the foyer. When cornered, Maggie blustered and tried to bluff her way out of a situation. ''There will be.'' He settled his garrison cap on his head at a rakish angle. ''Well, as they say, let's get this show on the road. I want to go Mach 3 with my hair on fire, Donovan.''

Chapter Three

During the ride over to the hangar area, Maggie said little because she was on a seesaw of emotion. They stopped at Ops and retrieved their flight gear, and she loosened up a little. Just getting to fly eased the tension that was always coiled tightly inside her. She'd been born that way. Flying was the only thing that erased her restlessness. Maggie always had to be moving, whether it was physically or mentally. Insomnia, upon occasion, was her best friend.

The truck delivered them to the hangar and Wes walked at her side, his duffel bag containing his helmet and oxygen mask slung across his left shoulder. He liked Maggie's flowing stride and those long legs of hers.

"How tall are you?" he asked.

"Five-eleven. You?"

"Six-five."

"You're a tall drink of water."

"Might say the same of you," he returned, catching her smile. Maggie was relaxing with every step toward the fighter sitting just outside the hangar doors. Wes saw her name just below the opened cockpit. Her air crew was waiting expectantly; the ladders were hooked alongside the fuselage so they could climb up into the double cockpit.

"A woman in your air crew?" Wes asked.

"Chantal Percival is my chief, and she's the best in the Navy, in my opinion. I fought hammer and tong to get her assigned to me and my jet when I got here. She's been with me the two years I've been at Miramar."

"Pretty lady," he mused. "That's an observation, Donovan, not a sexual comment." Even wearing a dark green T-shirt, which outlined her full breasts to perfection, Chantal was definitely a head turner.

Maggie remained silent. Then she introduced Wes to her air crew. Salutes and handshakes were exchanged. To her surprise, Chantal seemed immune to Wes's good looks and charm. How was that possible, when Maggie's own heart seemed completely attuned to his every word, look and smile? All business now, Maggie signed off the discrepancy log Chantal handed her, then made the visual walk-around inspection of her aircraft. In the meantime, Wes had climbed into the back seat and was getting help with his array of harnesses from one of her other ground-crew members.

Wes settled back, thanking the young petty officer who had helped him. The rear seat of a Tomcat was a familiar friend, and he strapped the knee board around his left thigh and began his preflight checklist. From time to time, though, he raised his helmeted head to observe Maggie in action.

In her cockpit, which was directly in front of his with his instrument panel between them, she tucked her red hair beneath the skullcap. Even after slipping on her helmet—white with a pair of red eagle wings painted on the front—she wouldn't be mistaken for a man. Wes smiled to himself and absorbed her profile as she gave last-minute instructions to Chantal, who stood on the ladder next to her. He hadn't realized how classic the line of her profile was until she turned.

Shaking himself internally, Wes decided there was a definite mystique to Maggie. Her features intrigued him. A man could spend the rest of his life mapping out her face and expressions and always be pleasantly surprised by something new about her. Few women had that kind of mystery.

Slow down, buddy. You just got out of a divorce that's still hurting you. Wes frowned and forced himself to concentrate on what he was doing. This was no time to resurrect his marriage, ex-wife or the light of his life, his daughter, Annie. Still, when Wes lifted his head and saw Maggie smile, his heart took off on its own flight as his mire of emotions suddenly dissolved beneath the warmth conveyed in her eyes and beautifully expressive mouth.

In no time, Maggie had the Tomcat anchored at the end of the runway, ready to take off. Dana and her

RIO, in another F-14, had taken off twenty minutes earlier. They would be "the enemy," stalking Maggie and Wes and trying to shoot them down over the restricted airspace north of the station. It would be up to Wes to spot them first and give Maggie the needed information to evade any surprise attack—and to give her the advantage that could enable her to "shoot down" Dana's aircraft electronically. Once a "kill" was registered, they would go on to the next test.

Wes listened idly to the control chatter. They were Red Dog 103 today, their call sign. He liked Maggie's firm, husky voice. Smiling beneath his oxygen mask, which was strapped tightly to his face, Wes brought down both the clear plastic and dark visor across his upper face. Both visors fit like a puzzle piece against the top of his oxygen mask. Maggie had done the same thing. Now they looked like genderless beings. Up in the air, Wes ruminated, tinkering with all his instruments to make sure they were up and operating properly, a person's sex really didn't matter at all. He was curious about Maggie's flying and combat ability.

"You ready back there, Bishop?"

"Roger."

"I'm requesting afterburner takeoff."

"To see if I can stand the heat in the kitchen?"

She laughed. "No. I know Dana Turcotte too well. She's liable to attack as soon as we get into the restricted airspace north of here, and I want all the altitude I can get. Go in high so you have the look-down, shoot-down advantage. If anyone's coming out of the sun, it's going to be us, not her."

Silently Wes applauded Maggie using "us" instead of "me." Good. She thought in terms of a team; wasn't ego bound like a lot of combat pilots. "Sounds good to me. Let's turn and burn."

What a difference between Hall and Wes! Maggie didn't say anything, concentrating fully on the forthcoming takeoff, with the F-14 shaking and howling around them. Compared to Hall, Wes sounded a hundred percent more confident in that rear seat. Hall was twenty-four. Bishop's five years of experience were already making her feel less edgy. Getting permission for takeoff, Maggie notched the twin throttles beneath her left hand into the afterburner range.

The sudden acceleration pinned her against the ejection seat, and Maggie smiled, relaxing beneath the incredible G's as they built up. Cat screamed down the runway, feeling solid beneath her hands and feet. The F-14 was the Navy's premier fighter, an unequaled tool in the military arsenal. The sleek twin-tailed fighter rotated smoothly beneath her gloved hand. In seconds, they were thundering straight up into the pale blue sky, clawing for thousands of feet of altitude within seconds.

Wes sat back and enjoyed the ride. In minutes they reached forty-five thousand feet, flying high above the California desert. He was already leaning forward, his eyes narrowed on the array of various radar screens in front of him. Each type of radar performed a different function, and much depended upon his alertness and experience in using them.

"How many minutes before we hit the restricted area?" Wes asked.

"Five minutes. Anything on the scopes?"

"No, clear."

"Dana's just about as sneaky as I am. Expect the unexpected with her."

"Okay. You said her last name was Turcotte?"

"Yes. Why?"

"When I got my first RIO assignment five and a half years ago, I flew with Griff Turcotte, the Turk."

"I'll be damned, you know Griff. Yeah, he and Dana have been married for two years now."

"I hope it's happier than his last marriage. He went through hell with his first wife."

"It's a happy, solid marriage from what I can tell."

"Good."

"How long did you and the Turk fly together?"

"Two years."

Maggie was constantly rubbernecking, revolving her head from left to right, her eyes scanning the flight instruments or hunting the sky above and around them for possible enemy aircraft. "Griff shot down one of those Libyan jets. Were you with him?"

"Yes."

Maggie nodded. Good, she had an RIO with combat experience. That couldn't hurt their chances at Red Flag, only improve them. She opened her mouth to ask him if he had anything on radar when he spoke up.

"Nothing on the scopes yet."

She smiled. "Are you a mind reader? I was just going to ask."

"Comes with the territory. No RIO wants his pilot on his back asking questions constantly. It interferes with my concentration."

"I like your style, Bishop." And she liked him. By now, Maggie had surrendered to whatever her body and heart were up to when it came to Wes. She was too busy flying and concentrating to try and explain her feminine responses to him.

"So far, I like yours, too."

"Let's take this one step at a time," Maggie warned, trying to keep the pleasure of his compliment out of her voice. Wes, she decided, was just one of those guys who was able to make personal contact with every person he met, making them feel special and wanted. That's all it was, Maggie thought, disheartened. "We're going to enter the restricted zone in thirty seconds."

"Roger. Thirty seconds." He tensed, his eyes glued to the radar screens.

Below them, Maggie could see the brown desert with the tiny dots of green here and there that were Joshua trees, cactus and hardy brush-type plants. Concentration intensified as her eyes flicked between her instruments and the sky around them.

"Got a bogey at five hundred feet coming up at us at two-four-zero. Thirty miles away."

"That's her!" Maggie quickly switched on her rocket and missile selectors. The HUD display lit up, a geometric crisscross of colored lines that gave her specific information on terrain as well as when she was in firing range.

This was almost too easy, Maggie thought. Dana was showing herself too early. Bishop kept up his information to her, keeping her filled in on the situation so she could make proper assessment. At twenty miles, she electronically signaled the firing of a Sparrow. It was a heat seeker, so Dana, in order to escape it, would have to do some avoidance flying.

"She's lost the Sparrow," Wes reported after a minute.

"Damn. That means we're going to have to go on deck and hunt her down the hard way."

"Afraid so."

"Hang on." Maggie banked the fighter and they gracefully arced from high altitude down to five hundred feet off the desert surface.

Wes watched from the back seat, fascinated with Maggie's hunter attitude. He knew a lot of pilots who would stay a long way away from their targets and just trade missiles with the enemy aircraft. Not her. She was going to flush out and hunt her "enemy" down. The thermals were pronounced, and the F-14 bumped and thumped along violently in the curtains of heat rising from the desert. The ground flashed by them, a blur of brown and green. The air turbulence became so bad that his teeth chattered, and it felt as if they were riding in a milk-shake machine. Still, Maggie held the fighter steady, snaking close to the ground, hunting out her adversary with the help of his radar screens and verbal information.

For three hours, they worked together and tested each other. When they landed back at Miramar, Wes ruefully noticed that the armpits of his flight suit were dark with perspiration. Maggie said little to him until they were on the ground and walking back to the hangar to hitch a ride to Ops. Dana had landed ahead of them and was already in a vehicle waiting for them.

"Great flight!" Dana congratulated Maggie. "You're a tiger at low altitude. I thought for sure I could hide behind those hills and outfox you."

Maggie climbed in and grinned, the warmth of the genuine compliment flowing through her. "Gotcha four out of five times."

"Not bad," Dana agreed with a laugh. Her RIO, Lieutenant Jeff Smith, shook hands with Wes.

Maggie introduced Wes to everyone and the van trundled slowly toward Ops. Wes sat supremely confident, seemingly unfazed by the rigorous three-hour flight she'd put him through. When he turned and looked over at Maggie, there was devilry in his eyes and he smiled.

It was a brazenly confident smile, and Maggie knew it. Still, his high spirits were infectious, and her mouth curved a bit in response. Dana, who sat behind her, placed a hand on her shoulder.

"Hey, don't forget, we're having dinner at Molly's tonight at 1900."

"Not to worry. I'd never forget a night Molly cooks."

"She's your other friend?" Wes guessed.

"Yes. A test-flight engineer who is six months pregnant. Molly works at Ops as a ground instructor in aeronautical physics. Dana and I are going to be 'aunts.' We can hardly wait."

Wes saw the enthusiasm leap into Maggie's eyes when she talked about her friend's pregnancy. Idly, he listened to the two women chat, collecting and gathering bits of information about Maggie.

After filling out the mandatory flight reports at Ops, Maggie leaned back in her seat at the same table with Wes in one of the debrief rooms on the first floor. "I want you to read my assessment on you before I hand it in to my boss, Commander Parkinson. I think that's only fair."

Wes nodded and took the report. He pushed his toward her. "Better read mine, too."

"Should I be worried about what you're going to say?" Maggie did care, she discovered, what Wes thought of her as a pilot. If only she could read his mind to see if those dancing blue highlights in his eyes when he looked at her were for her alone, or a look he bestowed on everyone.

"I could ask the same of you." Wes was curious how she rated his performance in the cockpit. More than anything, he wanted the chance to work with Maggie. She was one hell of a pilot behind the stick, woman or not.

With a shrug, Maggie leaned back in the chair, his report balanced on her knee. "You know you passed," she told him drolly.

"Yeah, I'm pretty good at what I do."

He saw her waiting for him to say something about her performance. "And so are you."

Relief flowed through Maggie, though she tried to hide it by lowering her head to read his report.

Wes smiled at her reaction, but said nothing. Afterward, they traded reports. Maggie got up, pleased about Wes's praise of her flying ability. "I'll take these to the commander and seal the deal." She came around the desk and offered her hand to him.

The urge to step forward and plant a long, hot kiss on Maggie's lips, instead, was very real for Wes. However, he gripped her hand and was pleased again by her firm, returning shake. Pushing an F-14 through tight maneuvers was physically demanding, so he shouldn't have been surprised by her strength. It only made Maggie more alluring.

"Let's celebrate," he found himself saying as he reluctantly released her hand. "Let me buy you a beer over at the O club."

Her fingers tingled where he'd touched them. Prickles arced up her hand and into her wrist and lower arm. Maggie was amazed and overwhelmed at the same time. Sure, men had kissed her, but Wes had merely reached out and shaken her hand. Her response to him was heated. Trying to recover, Maggie nodded and unconsciously touched the hand he'd shaken. A beer sounded heavenly. Flying at high altitude and on one-hundred-percent oxygen for hours on end always made flight personnel very thirsty afterward. And beer was the drink of choice after a long, demanding flight; the only thing that seemed to quench the thirst.

"I'll take you up on it. Thanks."

Inordinately pleased with himself, Wes glanced at his watch. They had two hours before Maggie was due at her friend's house for dinner. Good.

Maggie chose the quieter dining room to drink a beer with her new RIO. She received a number of gawking looks from fellow pilots as Wes walked past the bar area toward the dining room.

"I hope you know what you're in for, Bishop."

"Oh?"

"Yeah. Those jocks in there are going to tease you to death, now that you're flying with me."

"I've been known to take a couple of hits on the chin and live to tell about it. I think I'll survive anything they lob at me."

Maggie liked his laid-back approach to life. "Don't say I didn't warn you," she countered, then asked the hostess for a booth in a corner where they could have some privacy. At this time of day, few people were eating. The bar, however, was elbow to elbow with jocks.

After Wes ordered the beers and Maggie paid for them, he leaned forward and said, "Okay, tell me about yourself."

She sipped the beer, suddenly unable to relax. "I get jumpy when a guy starts hitting on me with twenty questions."

"This is different. I'm your RIO for the next three months."

"Do you always get what you want, Bishop?"

"No, but I try."

Chuckling, Maggie stretched her long legs out across the leather seat of the booth and relaxed. She supposed it didn't look very military or even socially acceptable to do it, but she didn't care. "I'm a pretty private person." Why did he want to know about her? Maggie shrugged the question off. Wes was the kind of guy who no doubt established a personal relationship with each person he had to work with. Somehow the realization was a blow to her heart.

"The Cherokee are like that, too," Wes said. "They don't like their pictures taken because they think it steals a part of their soul." He cocked his head, studying her. "Is that how you feel when talking about yourself?"

"You amaze me with your perception," Maggie replied, meaning it sincerely.

"As if men can't have some of what you women have?"

A smile tugged at her mouth. She drank some more of her beer and reached for the basket that contained chips and pretzels. "Caught red-handed."

"You're a little bit of a female chauvinist."

"Guilty as charged. I've got to try and watch that tendency."

"Who sold you a bill of goods that all men were insensitive to you as a human being?"

Maggie quirked her mouth. "Not my father, that's for sure. I came out of a family where women are looked upon as equals, Wes. There were four girls, and my parents taught us that we were just as strong, intelligent and capable as any man. Maybe it's the Celt blood in our veins—you know, over in England and Ireland, up through Roman times, our women fought as warriors beside their men."

Wes scratched his jaw, thinking about it. "I've got a degree in aeronautical engineering, but my worst course was history."

Pleased he held a degree in the same field that she did, Maggie nodded. "I'm sure in the next three months of working with me, you'll learn more about

the Irish than you ever wanted to know. I'm proud of
my heritage and what it's given me."

"I don't mind. Remember, I'm one-third Irish and
I know a lot about my Cherokee roots, because my
father was born and raised on the reservation. And my
mother steeped me in her Italian heritage, early on.
The Irish part of me is the only blank left to fill in.
You can help me with it."

Tearing her gaze from his eyes, Maggie found herself talking very quickly, a nervous habit of hers.
"We're a very different race genetically from other
women, I feel. Did you know that in a recent study
initiated by the three military academies, seventy percent of the women graduating from them were of Irish
descent?"

"Says something about their warriorlike ability,"
Wes pondered, sipping his beer.

Maggie raised a hand to her temple to try to tame
the loose tendrils. She was sure her hair was mussed
and badly in need of a brushing. With Wes, suddenly
she cared about her appearance—and was nonplussed by that discovery. "I genuinely feel that because our Celt and Druid ancestors approved and
promoted women fighting alongside the men, that the
characteristic was passed on to us genetically. I'm not
surprised by the academies' figures."

Running his fingers down the beaded, sweaty glass,
Wes held her gaze. How proud and fierce Maggie was
about her heritage. Wes had always believed that roots
gave one not only strength, but a feeling of wholeness
and connectedness. This had helped him at several
points in his own life.

"I'm curious, Maggie, about one thing," Wes murmured.

She liked the way her name rolled off his lips. It was tough not to stare like a schoolgirl at Wes because of his intense good looks. She tilted her head.

"Shoot."

"Are you saying Irishwomen are drawn to the military because they are born killers?"

Frowning, Maggie sat up. There was a teasing quality in the depths of his dark blue eyes. "I'm not comfortable with the term you used. Irishwomen have a powerful genetic memory of protection and defending home, family and country. That doesn't make them cold-blooded killers. Women in general, I feel, are the fabric that holds the family unit together. On a larger scale, the country they live in is simply an extension of their families. When something threatens their families, women tend to get territorial and even combative if the situation calls for it. Look at the French Resistance during World War II. Plenty of Frenchwomen worked right along with the men, taking the same risks. Russia had thousands of women soldiers and pilots. They fought the Germans, and died right alongside their men."

"So, you're saying that Irishwomen are defenders, not killers?"

"Yes. But, make no mistake: I would kill if necessary, if my home, family or country were threatened with destruction."

Wes nodded, holding her suddenly serious eyes, turned to a deep jade color with her intensity. "So, for you, there's a difference between killing for defensive purposes and cold-blooded murder? Even an enemy?''

''You really are a devil's advocate, aren't you?''

''I just want to know your thinking. Right now you're in a training program with the blessings of Congress, but you've never really been tested in combat. I wonder, when it does happen, how you'll react to it.''

''Many male pilots today don't have combat experience, either. So to me, it's a moot point, Wes. How did you handle knowing that you helped shoot down that Libyan MiG?''

His brows knitted. ''After we landed back on the carrier, there was a lot of celebrating, backslapping and congratulations. Later, in my quarters, I got sick to my stomach. Then I had nightmares—and did a lot of soul-searching about killing a man who probably had left a wife and children behind....''

An ache rose in Maggie's throat. She saw the anguish in Wes's face. ''I couldn't ever take joy from killing someone,'' Maggie whispered. ''But if I had to in the role of defending my country, I'd do it.'' She rubbed her brow and gave him a glance. ''And I'm very sure I'd have the same reaction you did. Thanks for leveling with me. Most of these jocks around here beat their chests like gorillas about how tough they are, but my instincts tell me they'd have second thoughts about killing another pilot, too.''

''It's called remorse,'' Wes told her dryly. ''And it's a part of our business. The sordid side of it. There are a few combat pilots who I'd consider cold-blooded killers, who feel that taking another life is sanctioned without need for remorse, guilt or soul-searching, but most of them would probably be in my category."

With a grimace, Maggie agreed. She placed her mug on the table. "I just hope I never have to kill anyone."

"Just about every guy feels the same way, but most wouldn't admit it."

"That's nice to know. Sure skews the image the military has with the civilian populace, doesn't it?"

Wes smiled. "Roger that."

"So you said you were divorced and have a daughter?" Maggie probed, again surprised by her sudden personal questions. She'd never asked Hall things like this.

"Yes." He leaned down and unzipped one of the pant-leg pockets of his flight suit and withdrew a wallet. "Here's a picture of Annie." Wes couldn't keep the pride out of his voice. "She's five. The woman holding her is my ex-wife, Jenny."

"Your daughter sure has your eyes and mouth."

"Thanks." He smiled shyly. "Annie has some of my Cherokee genes, I think. The rest of her takes after Jenny."

The woman in the picture was blond and blue-eyed. In Maggie's opinion, small and frail looking. In some ways, she reminded her of Molly. But Molly's face had inherent strength in it. Jenny's did not. The black-haired girl in her arms was just as pretty as her mother. Maggie could see why Wes was so proud of his daughter.

"You made a handsome family, Wes."

"Thanks." He shrugged. "Navy life didn't agree with Jenny."

"The months away at sea?" Maggie guessed.

"Yes. You know how a military wife has to be self-sufficient and handle the emergencies when we're away. Jenny just couldn't do it. I wasn't there when Annie was born. That's when our marriage started down a long road I'd just as soon forget." Wes shook his head. "The straw that broke the camel's back was when I was gone on a six-month Med cruise a year ago and Annie got appendicitis. She had to have emergency surgery. I wasn't there for that, either. Jenny came apart. She got hysterical thinking Annie was going to die. There was no one there to hold Jenny, support her or take over."

Maggie felt for his ex-wife. "I feel like that sometimes myself. As much as I'd like to believe I can overcome every obstacle life throws at me, I sometimes wonder about it."

"Oh?"

"So far, I've been successful at everything I've ever attempted, Wes. Some people say I'm lucky, others say I've got a charmed life."

"Irish luck, by any chance?"

She smiled. "Not in my opinion. It's called hard work and more hard work. I'm driven, in case you didn't know."

"You're like a tightly wound spring."

"No hiding secrets from you, is there?"

"We don't need secrets between us," he offered. "We're a team, remember? We depend on each other to survive up in the air. With the exception of marriage, I don't know how much closer you can get to a person than an RIO is to a pilot."

He was right. "Well, as I was saying, I'm an over-achiever and I've gotten everything I ever went after."

"You've never failed?"

"That's right. My folks raised us to be successful. There was no room for failure."

With a grin, Wes said, "Must be nice. I've fallen down, busted my nose and butt a few times and found egg on my face more than I'd care to admit."

She laughed and lightly traced the bridge of her nose. "I've had a broken nose, too. So we're even."

"Who hit you?" Wes imagined Maggie was a hellion in the making even back in grade school, taking no guff from any young punk who might have tried to push her the wrong way.

"I did it myself. I took a dare from a ten-year-old boy that I could swing like Tarzan from one tree to another. I told him Jane was better at it than Tarzan ever could be—I was a feminist even at ten." She laughed. "The long and short of it was, the rope I used was old and frayed. Halfway there, it broke and I fell thirty feet to the ground. When I regained conscious-ness ten minutes later I found out I had a broken nose and jaw." She touched the left side of her face, indi-cating where the break had occurred. The look of concern and then care on Wes's face surprised her. There was genuine compassion in his eyes.

"Hey, it was no big deal. I got my jaw wired shut for six weeks, had fun learning to drink my meals through a straw and got a more interesting-looking nose as a result."

"Yeah, but you were only ten years old. When Annie's hurt, she likes to crawl into my arms and be held afterward. Did someone hold you, Maggie?"

Touched, she shrugged. "My mother marched me off to the emergency room and sat with me. That's as close to getting held as I got. I went home and went to my bedroom and slept the rest of the day. The next day, I was out playing with the kids in the neighborhood again. You couldn't keep a Donovan down long."

Maggie was in need of a little personal care and attention. Wes said nothing, holding on to that discovery. "Still, children need to be held a lot and loved—to know they've got a safe place to go to when they're hurting or in trouble. So do adults."

Glancing at her watch, Maggie said regretfully, "No argument from me. I've got to take off or my mother-to-be, Molly, is going to bust my chops for being late for one of her fabulous dinners." More than anything, Maggie wanted to stay with Wes and talk. He made it easy to open up and share personal stories about her life. She stood, realizing it was the first time she'd wanted to share so much with a man.

Wes rose, too. "Does she cook for you?"

"The three of us trade cooking duties on a weekly basis like we did back at Pensacola. Dana and I love it when it's Molly's turn to cook. She's the best of all of us. I think tonight she's having seafood Newburg on popovers."

Wes's mouth watered. "God, that sounds good."

Maggie couldn't help but notice the fervency in his voice. She almost invited him to come with her, but wasn't sure of her friend's reaction. She knew Molly got upset if there wasn't enough food to go around, and she rarely made extra portions. Maybe some other time she would invite Wes along. She'd ask Molly about it tonight. As Maggie and Wes left the O club, she asked him, "What will you do for dinner tonight?"

"Probably grab a TV dinner at my apartment."

She winced. "You're as bad as I am. I live on those things, too."

Laughing, Wes reached out and briefly touched her shoulder. He hadn't meant to, but the reaction was spontaneous. As his hand rested on her proud shoulder, he said, "One of us needs to learn how to cook, Maggie."

His touch was shocking, pleasurable. Maggie held her breath for a moment, and in her mind, she wondered what it would be like to kiss his smiling mouth. Heat zigzagged through her from head to toe over that sizzling thought. Disgruntled at her meandering thoughts, she tried to recover. "I'll buy you the cookbooks and cheer you on, Bishop. How's that sound?"

"We'll see...." So, Maggie liked him. Wes had sensed the personal chemistry between them since the moment they'd met. When he'd unthinkingly touched her, he saw her lovely eyes go wide with shock and then something else. Desire? Suddenly his life—at rock bottom for the past year—was looking a little brighter. Hope threaded through his heart as he walked her to the parking lot.

"What's on the agenda for tomorrow?"

Her pulse was bounding like a jet out of control. Did he hear the wobble in her voice? "Be at my office at 0800 and I'll lay out our Red Flag training program for you."

"I'll bring the doughnuts if you'll make the coffee, Donovan."

Maggie stopped beside her bright red Mazda Miata sports car. "I think it'd be safer for me to buy the doughnuts and *you* make the coffee."

He halted, throwing his hands on his hips. "You're *that* bad a cook?"

"Ask Molly and Dana sometime. The week it's my turn to cook, I buy frozen TV dinners for all of us every evening."

With a shake of his head, Wes laughed. "You're one of a kind, Maggie Donovan. One of a kind." And sweet God, how he reveled in her strength and confidence that shone like a beacon from her proud form.

"I just hope you can tolerate it for three months, Bishop." Maggie raised her hand. "See you tomorrow morning."

He gave her a lazy salute. "Roger."

Chapter Four

"Maggie, I just heard that your new RIO, Wes Bishop, is sinfully good-looking. Is he?" Molly placed the last of the steaming-hot dishes on the table where her two friends sat.

Digging eagerly into the seafood Newburg, Maggie looked across the table at Dana. "You've been filling her in, no doubt."

With a shrug, Dana murmured, "I was excited for you, and Moll practically dragged everything out of me, kicking and screaming." Dana flashed an impish smile in Molly's direction.

"Dana, that's not true! You came in here all agog over Wes Bishop, telling me he was a hunk," Molly protested primly.

Maggie ate with a vengeance. Combat-practice flights always made her ravenous.

"Well?" Molly prodded. "Do you like this new guy?"

"Better qualify that, Moll," advised Dana. "Do you mean as an RIO or as a hunk?"

"You two," Maggie muttered between bites, "are nosy snoops."

"No, we're not." Molly giggled. She spooned the steamed cauliflower sprinkled with light dill sauce onto her plate. "Besides, I can tell you like him on a personal level because you're blushing, Maggie Donovan."

"I don't blush."

"Gee, must be red beet stain she got into, then," Dana whispered conspiratorially over to Molly.

"But I didn't make beets for dinner."

"Very funny." Maggie sat back, her fork in one hand, her knife in the other. "You're both plotting against me, I can just feel it."

"Well," Dana said innocently, "you're the only one in the Sisterhood who's still single. Maybe we'd like to see you happy like us."

"I don't need a man to make me happy," Maggie replied through gritted teeth.

"Dana didn't say that. Women are perfectly capable of being happy without being married. It's just that—" Molly hesitated, searching for the right words "—I've seen how much more happy we've become with the right partner in our lives. We'd like the same for you, Maggie."

"So you're conspiring to doing a little matchmaking?" Maggie raised one eyebrow. "Bishop is my RIO. That's all. Nothing more."

"I hear he's divorced," Dana put in, a small smile stealing across her mouth.

"And he can stay that way!" Maggie's nostrils flared. "Brother, you two are like harpy eagles when you want something, aren't you?"

Molly giggled again. "Why don't you invite him over for dinner some night and let us meet him, Maggie? I'm sure he's like every other bachelor pilot: living on TV dinners."

"I was right: you are harpy eagles."

"Come on, Maggie. Climb down off your injured high horse and bring him over." Then Dana added, "We promise not to matchmake. Okay?"

Zeroing in on her two friends, who were giving her their best guileless looks, Maggie muttered, "You'd better not, or I'll wring your necks."

"Ohh, I love it when Maggie gets her hackles up! Don't you, Moll? She sounds so fierce!"

"You have more beet juice on your cheeks, Maggie," Molly pointed out.

"All right! All right, I'll invite him over just to get you two off my back! I can't stand this two-against-one routine. And I sure as hell don't want to go through this every night this week. Is tomorrow soon enough?"

Molly smiled sweetly. "Is he a meat-and-potatoes man? Or does he prefer gourmet cooking?"

"How the hell do I know?"

"Usually if you like a guy, you get a sixth sense about things like that," Dana explained, her grin widening.

Ducking her head and pretending to pay attention only to the food on her plate, Maggie refused to answer. It was embarrassing to be so transparent to her closest friends. Yes, she liked Wes on a personal level, but Maggie was sure it was only a one-way street. Wes was here because he liked the challenge of Red Flag and the idea of flying with a woman, that's all. "If I didn't like your cooking so much, Molly, I wouldn't show my face here for the rest of the week, until you two decide to lay off me."

"But I know how much you love my cooking. Wonderful! We'll expect Wes tomorrow night. Same time. Okay?"

Maggie glared at Molly. "Fine."

"We promise we'll be good," Dana told her.

"Sure, you will. You're like foxes in a henhouse. And dammit, I'm the hen this time!"

"Maggie, you're many things, but never a hen," Dana teased.

"More like a badger," Molly suggested grandly.

"Closer to a grouchy old mother bear who's been awakened during hibernation," Dana decided dryly. And then she broke into gales of unrestrained laughter.

Maggie squirmed in her seat. Her friends were astute, and she trusted their judgment in many areas. But this was the first time they'd zeroed in on her love life. Or, more accurately, on the lack of it. All her time and energy had been devoted to flying and training.

While they lingered over dessert—apple pie with vanilla ice cream—Dana again brought up the topic of Wes. They sat around in the living room on Molly's bamboo furniture. A black lacquered coffee table was the room's centerpiece, topped by a large silk-flower arrangement in a delicate Chinese vase.

Maggie, dressed in shorts and a blouse, sat on the carpeted floor. She leaned against the couch, dessert in hand. When she saw Dana studying her, she growled, "Okay, what's on your mind? It's written all over your face, Dana."

"I was just wondering how you got along with Bishop today, that's all."

Scowling, Maggie said, "In the cockpit, fine. He gives me a constant verbal status on what he sees on his scopes and lets me make the final decision on what we'll do."

"Just the opposite of Hall," Dana observed. "Good."

Molly tucked her feet beneath her. She sat on the couch next to Maggie. "Dana thought he was pretty nice."

"Yes, he's nice," Maggie agreed. "To everyone. It's his style, his way of getting along with others. That's all."

"I didn't mean that as a matchmaking comment."

"Sure?" Maggie smiled slightly.

"Very sure."

Maggie filled them in on her conversations with Wes. Both her friends had inordinately pleased looks on their faces when she'd finished. After getting up and serving coffee, Maggie came and sat down, a steaming mug in her hands.

"I just hope Bishop can stand the heat in the kitchen," Maggie told them. "Hall is stationed here, and will take every opportunity to tell him all kinds of untrue things about me."

"You've got to trust Bishop to sort through those things," Molly said.

With a quirk of her mouth, Maggie sighed. "I'm not very good at trusting a man with anything. That's part of the reason Hall and I butted heads. I come out of a family where women ruled the roost. They're smart, savvy and know how to move and shake things better than most men."

Dana nodded. "I agree with you that women have it over men in just about every case. But your up-bringing is going to work against you sometimes, Maggie. I think it's fine that your parents instilled the four of you with those beliefs. But I don't think they taught you much about compromise or trusting someone other than yourself to get a job done."

"Touché." Maggie sighed. "Yeah, if I'm going to make this thing work with Bishop, I've got to try and trust him."

Molly reached over, patting Maggie's shoulder. "The Irish are a proud people, Maggie. And you have a right to feel that way. But pride is expendable. It has to be, in order to get along in this world."

"It's either that," Dana added, "or run yourself into a brick wall because you're too stiff-necked to see the other side of an issue."

"I already screwed up with Hall," Maggie admitted. "I only hope I can be more sensitive to Bishop and pace myself better with him."

"I think you will." Dana smiled gently. "He likes you and vice versa. I think as a result, you'll both overlook some of each other's faults and weaknesses."

Maggie's heart took a leap at her friend's assessment. Could she be right? No. Impossible. No man she'd worked with since joining the Navy had ever looked at her as more than a sexless robot up in the front seat of an F-14. With a growl, Maggie got to her feet. "You don't give up, do you?" She went to the kitchen and placed her empty mug on the drain board. Returning to the living room, she found both her friends smiling up at her. They were tolerant smiles— the sort of smile a loving mother would give her errant child. At moments like this, Maggie did feel like the odd person out. She was the only one without a "significant other." Shaking her head, she picked up her purse and headed for the door.

"Thanks for dinner. I'll see you two tomorrow at the station."

"Remember, dinner's at 1800," Molly called.

"How could I forget?" Maggie opened the screen door and turned to Molly. "What are you going to have? I know Bishop will want to know."

"Umm, let's see. How about roast leg of lamb, cranberry-grape salad and potatoes au gratin, with chocolate cake for dessert? Think that'll entice him?"

With a roll of her eyes, Maggie replied, "He'll probably want to marry you on the spot, Molly. Sounds great. See ya...."

Wes was in Maggie's office when she arrived next morning. She'd brought the doughnuts and, sure enough, he'd made coffee in the small pot sitting on a shelf teetering with books and files. Pleasantly surprised by her appearance, he smiled a good-morning to her. Her hair, which had been mussed yesterday, was smoothly combed and tamed into a chignon at the nape of her neck. Her feathery bangs barely brushed her arched brows while curled tendrils trailed from her temples. He was even more surprised to see her nails painted, and a hint of perfume wafted around him as she entered.

There was no doubt that she was a very feminine woman, even though she operated in a very male world. The thought pleased him immensely, and for no concrete reason.

He liked the sprinkling of copper-colored freckles across Maggie's cheeks. They gave her face a touch of childlike innocence. As he sat there, he mused again that Maggie's precarious position in the Red Flag program had weighed her down with more responsibility than he'd want to carry himself. As he watched her stow her briefcase beneath her desk and scare up mugs for their coffee, Wes was struck by the fact that he'd rarely seen Maggie smile.

"You ever do something crazy every once in a while?" he asked suddenly.

Maggie glanced around at him in surprise. Since entering the office, her pulse seemed out of control— again. Trying to hide her nervousness, she poured their coffee and handed him a mug. "Like what?"

"Since entering the Navy, have you ever pulled any crazy stunts? You know, acted like a kid when you got the chance."

Maggie sat down at her desk, doughnut in one hand, coffee in the other. It was 0700 and most of the Top Gun personnel were arriving at Ops. "No." Just having the pleasure of gazing at Wes was like a gift to Maggie. Frustrated with her uncontrolled response to him, she tried to stuff it deep down inside herself. Those feelings had no place here in the office. "Why?"

Wes shrugged, reaching for the sack that contained the doughnuts. "Just wondered." The strain around her eyes and mouth was telling. Too much responsibility, too much pressure had made her all adult; and her ability to be a child, to laugh and relax, had been pushed aside by those demands. "With your red hair and those big green eyes, you look like the type to get into trouble every now and then."

"I've worked very hard these last six years at staying out of trouble and keeping my nose clean, Bishop. Being the first woman combat-pilot doesn't invite screw-ups." She shook her head. "No, I don't do crazy things."

"Hmm, that's too bad." Wes understood her reasoning. He'd lain awake last night thinking about Maggie. Maybe *feeling* was a better word to use. He was fascinated by her blend of strength, courage and femininity. Few women gave themselves permission to be all those things in today's society, Wes reflected. Maggie was a symbol in more ways than perhaps she even realized.

Maggie was very special in his eyes—and in his heart. One of a kind.

"By the way, my friend, Lieutenant Molly Rutledge Sinclair, has invited you over for dinner tonight. She took pity on you when I told her you ate TV dinners just like I do."

He grinned. "Real food?"

She smiled, mesmerized by the shape of his mouth and that lazy curve that deepened when he was pleased about something. "Yeah. Want to come?" Her heart did a crazy flip-flop in her breast at the thought that he might turn down the invitation. Maggie found herself fighting the need to drop the formality and just be herself with Wes. She'd done that with Hall, and it had reaped dangerous results. Still, when his blue eyes danced with merriment, her smile broadened.

"Sure. Thanks for taking pity on this poor bachelor, all alone here in San Diego."

"Save the sob story, Bishop. It doesn't wash with me. All you guys want to play on a woman's heartstrings—make us think you're helpless out there in the big, bad world without a woman in your bed and cooking for you."

Raising his hands in a sign of peace, Wes laughed. "Ouch!"

Finishing off her doughnut, Maggie wiped her fingers on a napkin. Was she in the midst of a heart attack, or was her pulse always going to do flip-flops when Wes was around? "Ready to get down to business?"

Nodding, Wes got up and came around to her side of the desk as she cleared off a space for the book containing the training schedule. He placed one hand on her chair and the other on the desk. Leaning over her shoulder, he stood and listened to Maggie's presentation of what was expected of both of them for the next month. They'd be flying every day, chalking up two to three hours at a crack, sharpening their individual skills on very carefully conceived flights.

"Who made up these flights?" he wanted to know.

Maggie's eyes widened considerably when he came around the desk to stand inches from where she sat. She could feel the heat from his body, the strength of him as a man. Her mouth suddenly dry, she croaked, "Molly and I."

"They're demanding, but good," Wes congratulated her.

"Tell Molly that tonight and she'll give you second helpings of dessert."

Grinning, Wes said nothing. Although he enjoyed home cooking as much as anyone, Maggie interested him far more than food. He tried to keep his focus on what was being outlined, but Maggie's soft hint of perfume, her lean but graceful fingers moving in ballerina fashion across the schedule, and her simple closeness, all conspired against him.

As she flipped the page of the schedule to the second month of training, Wes watched the fluorescent lights dance off Maggie's hair, bringing out the deep, wine-colored highlights and gold and crimson colors.

He had to physically stop himself from touching those thick, shining strands. What would it be like to ease the pins from her chignon and allow that mass of barely tamed hair to flow and cascade through his fingers? The thought was heated, filled with promise. On its heels came a discouraging realization: Maggie might already have a man in her life.

Frowning, Wes divided his attention between Maggie and his own feelings. First of all, why was he entertaining a personal relationship with her when he'd been in a dead zone since his divorce? Was there room in his life for a relationship? He was unsure of the answer. In three months, he'd be out to sea for another three months of the cruise before he came back to San Diego. And from experience, he knew relationships died on the vine when a man was away for so long. That's how he'd lost Jenny and Annie. The hurt and loss from that was too much for Wes to want to repeat it.

Trying to force his feelings aside, Wes knew he didn't dare get involved with Maggie. It just wasn't worth the emotional price to either of them. He'd barely survived the divorce and losing his daughter. His heart was still too scarred and tender. Deep down, Wes knew he was acting like a coward, afraid to reach out to love again, for fear of losing again. Whatever kind of courage it took to do that, evidently he didn't possess it. That realization hurt.

"What's this?" Brad Hall boomed from the office entrance. He pressed his hands against the door frame and grinned. "My, aren't we cozy. You never let me that close to you, Donovan. Must be love at first sight."

Wes felt Maggie tense. Instantly he straightened and placed his hand on her shoulder—a signal that he'd handle Hall.

Feeling immediately guilty, as if she'd been caught in an act of intimacy, not business, Maggie snapped back, "Cut the crap, Brad. We're working."

Hall frowned and thrust his hands on his hips. "This will make great gossip down at the locker room, Wes. Better watch it. She eats men for breakfast, lunch and dinner."

Fury shot through Maggie and she opened her mouth to fire back a salvo at Hall. Instead, Wes's hand increased its pressure on her shoulder. She looked up at him. His face was placid, but she saw the anger in his eyes. For the first time in her life, Maggie felt protected, suddenly trusting Wes to deal with the situation.

"Not in my book," Wes said smoothly. "Besides, I don't think Maggie's the problem."

Hall snorted and grinned. "I suppose I'm at fault?"

Wes returned the smile, but it didn't reach his eyes. "I've met a lot of men who are threatened by a woman in one of our slots. Check it out, buddy."

With a laugh, Brad turned and left.

"That mealymouthed—"

"Now, Red, he's not worth it."

Red. Maggie shot a look at Wes, wildly aware that his hand was still on her shoulder. Oddly it felt right, and she absorbed his touch as if she were starved for such contact. She also liked his nickname for her. The anger that had accumulated in her dissolved beneath Wes's coaxing look.

"You're right," she muttered, trying to refocus her attention on the schedule. How could she, with his hand on her shoulder? Closing her eyes, Maggie took a deep, steadying breath.

Wes had to remind himself to take his hand off Maggie. He liked the firm feel of her muscles beneath her flight suit. He longed to simply run his fingers across her shoulder and explore her—all of her. Shaken by the powerful need, Wes frowned at himself. "Men like Hall act like little boys when they get around a woman who's confident. Just ignore him."

"That's easier to do now that I don't fly with the jerk."

Replacing his hand on the back of her chair, Wes leaned over Maggie again. "He's immature upon occasion. Hall was with my squadron on board the carrier last year, and although he's good at what he does, it's gone to his head."

"No kidding." Maggie had the insatiable urge to slam the schedule book closed and do something wild and crazy with Wes. She wondered what it would be like to go to the Pacific Ocean, which wasn't that far away, and just walk with him on the beach and enjoy the day. With a doleful shake of her head, she whispered, "Let's get back to work."

The nickname for Maggie had just slipped out of Wes. As he forced his attention back to the schedule, he wondered darkly where "Red" had come from. He'd felt the immediate tension in her when Hall challenged them. Great. His protective mechanism was working overtime. But his calling her Red had sounded more like an endearment than the kind of name one flying buddy gives another. No, the name had rolled off his lips with warmth and care. Damn. Under no circumstances could Wes allow his healing heart to reach out. Not now. It wouldn't be fair to him or to Maggie. They had only three months together, and then he'd be torn from the fabric of her world. Double damn!

Maggie's hands were sweaty. They had been since Wes had entered her apartment. She chastised herself as she quickly changed out of her flight uniform and into a pair of hot-pink shorts and a flowery print blouse in wine, pink and gold. Slipping into a pair of sandals, she grabbed her small white purse and went to the living room where Wes was waiting for her. Next stop was his apartment before heading to Molly's for dinner.

Wes looked up as Maggie appeared in the living-room doorway. Heat rushed through him at the sight of her hair flowing free across her shoulders. The bright red strands curled slightly, gleaming crimson and gold in the room's natural light. An ache centered in him, and Wes's eyes narrowed in appreciation. God, how pretty Maggie was! She was all gorgeous legs, with her hips nicely rounded. Civilian attire did nothing but emphasize her fluid, graceful beauty.

"No one would ever think you were a combat pilot," he managed to croak.

Heat swept into Maggie's face. She groaned inwardly. The look in Wes's eyes was pure, unadulterated hunger—for her. A sizzling fire arced through Maggie, and she halted beneath his smoldering inspection. Unprepared for his honest reaction to her as a woman, Maggie found herself savoring the feeling—a feeling she didn't have often.

Trying to recover, she shrugged delicately. "Can't believe everything you hear about us women military pilots, can you?" If only she'd stop blushing! My God, she never blushed! But Wes Bishop's thoroughly masculine appraisal had caught her completely off guard. Maggie had grown used to the lascivious looks military men had given her over the years. But Wes's response of genuine appreciation rattled her composure. His look was more than appraisal; there was a hungry, seething fire in his narrowed blue eyes, and the way he set his mouth made her go shaky inside.

Wes jerked his gaze away from Maggie, totally displeased with the way he'd reacted. "Women pilots are still women," he managed to say. He turned and walked toward the screen door where the sunlight spilled in across the green-carpeted floor. Somehow, he had to get himself under control. It was obvious Maggie saw his hunger for her, and that she was no less affected than he was. Her vulnerability made her that much more enticing to Wes.

Maggie said little as Wes drove to his apartment, a couple of miles from hers. The sun was on the western horizon, the sky dark blue and cloudless. She felt tension around Wes, but wasn't she shaken, too? All she'd done was put on civilian clothes. The change in her couldn't be *that* dramatic. What had sparked his reaction?

Wes's apartment was small but tastefully furnished. Maggie moved nervously around the cream-carpeted living room, running her fingers idly across the back of an early American-style maple couch. Upset by his reaction to her, she was no longer hungry. And on top of everything else, Maggie knew she still had to endure a long, drawn-out dinner with her two friends ogling and making innuendos. With a roll of her eyes, she wondered how she was going to survive the evening.

Wes reappeared dressed in a pair of belted ivory chino slacks and a light green, short-sleeved cotton shirt. He gave Maggie a slight smile.

"Ready?"

"Sure." She tried not to stare at him, but it was impossible. How brazenly male, how utterly beautiful Wes was, no matter what he wore. It made her heart beat solidly in her chest. "Civilian clothes look good on you, too," Maggie muttered as she went out the front door.

Laughing, Wes followed her down the marigold-lined sidewalk to the rear parking lot where his black Toyota Celica sports car sat. "What you mean is we both clean up pretty well."

His laughter broke the unbearable thread of tension in Maggie. She managed a smile as he opened the passenger door for her. "You could pass for a magazine model, Bishop."

Wes got into the driver's seat and shut the door. He traded a wry glance with Maggie. "As if you couldn't, too."

The smoldering heat was back in his narrowed cobalt-blue eyes. Maggie drew in a ragged breath. She had never thought of herself in those terms. She fastened her seat belt and sat back. Wes's compliment overflowed with hidden messages, all of them filled with sensual promise. Never had she felt more feminine, more aware of herself as a woman.

Chapter Five

Maggie had accurately predicted Molly's innocent reaction to Wes Bishop. She simply stood gawking up at him. Embarrassed, Maggie hugged her very pregnant friend, then went out to the kitchen to help her with the last-minute preparations. Dana kept Wes entertained in the living room by pouring him a glass of Burgundy.

"He's a hunk!" Molly whispered fiercely, placing the roast leg of lamb on a huge platter.

"Looks mean absolutely nothing in the cockpit, and you know it."

Molly giggled and placed the platter in Maggie's hands. "You must have got close to the beet juice again, Maggie."

With a groan, Maggie left for the dining room.

Dana adroitly seated Maggie next to Wes at the table. Maggie could have killed her two friends at that point. Both had angelic expressions on their faces, but she felt like a bug under a microscope. Those two particular sets of inquiring eyes and ears missed nothing.

Later, in the living room, they all lounged around with dessert. Molly was sitting in her favorite chair, a maple rocker where she planned to rock her baby after its birth. Her dessert plate was balanced on her belly. Maggie had purposely sat on the floor next to the rocker; Wes and Dana were opposite them on the couch. Being so close to Wes at the table had made her nervous as hell. The man oozed charm and diplomacy. He had been a wonderful dinner companion, Maggie had to admit sourly. If only she hadn't blushed throughout the meal!

"So, tell me about your daughter, Annie," Molly pleaded.

Wes beamed. He withdrew his wallet and walked over to where Molly was seated, placing a photo in her extended hand. Molly kept the other hand on her plate so it wouldn't slip off while she looked at the picture.

"Even at five, Annie's a looker," Wes told her proudly.

"Isn't she, though! What lovely blue eyes." Molly looked up at Wes. "The same color as yours."

"Yeah," he admitted shyly. "Annie does take after me in some ways."

"You know our baby is going to be a girl, don't you?"

"No, I didn't."

Molly handed him back the picture. "The only bad thing is Cam's going to be at sea with his squadron when I have her."

Frowning, Wes tucked the photo back into his wallet. "That's too bad. Jenny, my ex-wife, was alone when she had Annie. I hated being away when that happened."

Maggie saw the anguish in Wes's eyes and heard the tremble in his voice. It touched her deeply. Few men were able to show their feelings as he did.

"I know," Molly commiserated softly. "Cam will never feel Rachel kick in my belly, and that hurts so much. All I can do is write and tell him about it, share it with him that way."

Maggie was studying Molly's translucent features, thinking how lovely she'd become with the pregnancy, when suddenly the plate on her belly jumped and slid.

With a cry, Molly tried to grab the plate, but it was too late. The cake crumbs and plate landed in Maggie's lap.

"Oh, dear..."

"No, it's okay, Molly." Maggie laughed, starting to pick up the crumbs around her. When Wes crouched down to help, she was wildly aware of his powerful masculine frame close to her.

"I'm sorry. Rachel kicks a lot at this time of night. Are you okay?"

"I'm fine. I've never seen that happen before," Maggie admitted with a smile. "My mother told me about it, but seeing it is something else." She saw the abject apology in Molly's hazel eyes, and Maggie's heart went out to her. "Really, everything's fine."

Wes picked up crumbs here and there and placed them back on the plate Maggie now held. "That was impressive, Molly." He leaned back on his heels, a wistful look on his face. "I never got to feel Annie kick like that, either. She was three months old when I got in off fleet duty."

"Then come here and feel her!" Molly gestured for Wes to give her his hand.

Maggie watched Wes's face as Molly placed his large hand across her swollen belly. His eyes turned a soft blue, and the curve of his mouth deepened with gratitude. There was such awe in his face as Rachel continued to kick beneath his hand.

"Feel her?" Molly asked excitedly, her hand across Wes's large, hairy one.

"Yeah..."

"Wonderful, isn't it? Just imagine, she's alive in there. I just love it every time she moves. Oh, my back aches sometimes, and I get more tired than usual, but I look forward to these times when Rachel's awake and moving around."

Wes nodded, his gaze straying to Maggie, who still sat beside the rocker. Her green eyes were warm with a tenderness that shook him to his soul. No longer was she the woman combat-pilot carrying responsibilities far beyond what anyone should bear, but a woman responding like a woman.

"Want to feel?" Wes asked Maggie.

Maggie grinned and eagerly set the plate aside, getting to her knees. Wes moved his hand and Maggie laid her hand across Molly's belly. To her utter surprise, Wes put his hand over hers.

Molly smiled warmly. "Having a baby is the most beautiful experience I've ever had, Maggie. Can you feel Rachel?"

"Yes..." Her heart was beating rapidly in counterpoint because Wes's hand was covering her own. His fingers were long, and curiously beautiful in a very male way. And there was such heat throbbing upward from her hand, and throughout her body at the intimate contact with him. She suddenly pulled her hand away, feeling as if she'd been burned, feeling unable to deal with the gamut of emotions he'd triggered in her with his spontaneous gesture.

"Thanks, Molly," Maggie whispered, getting to her feet. She quickly left the room, taking the plate to the kitchen. Her hands on the drain board, she bowed her head and tried to get a hold of her wildly arcing emotions. The need to simply turn around and find herself in Wes's arms was overpowering. What would it be like to kiss his so-very-male mouth? What would his eyes look like if she made passionate hungry love with him?

Touching her brow with her trembling hand, Maggie dragged in a deep breath of air. The poignancy of Wes's reaction to Rachel's kicking was undeniable. In that moment, Maggie realized just how much Wes loved Annie, and how much he lamented missing her birth. More than anything, she applauded his ability to show his feelings without apology. What a unique human being he was turning out to be—one wonderful surprise after another. These discoveries were all affecting Maggie very deeply. How was she going to continue to hide her own growing feelings toward him?

On the way back to her apartment, Maggie remained silent as Wes drove. It was nearly 2200, and darkness had settled in on the West Coast. Around them shone lights from the homes perched up on the rocky, desert hills of Poway.

"You're awfully quiet," Wes observed.

Maggie stirred, her emotions in a jumble over the past hour's excitement and happiness. "I guess I'm more tired than I thought," she lied softly.

"Yeah, the last couple of days have been rough on you."

She laid her head against the seat and tilted a glance in his direction. "On you, too."

"I'm tough. I can take it."

With a short laugh, Maggie said, "Here we go again with that double-standard fare."

"No," Wes countered seriously. "It *has* been harder on you. I've had the chance to see what you've been carrying, the responsibility on you. There's a lot at stake here, and the ball's been in your court for two years now. I'm just walking in for a three-month stint. That's nothing compared to the weight you've got on your shoulders."

Maggie was pleased with his insight. "Are you this understanding with everyone? Or just with me?"

"I try to be with everybody. Doesn't always work, but I try." Wes grinned. "Besides, for special people, I go to special lengths."

Maggie's heart sank and despair settled in. It was just as she'd thought: Wes was warm and charming with everyone. She really wasn't one of those "special people" he was talking about—sure that he meant his ex-wife, and his beautiful daughter. Maggie shook her head. "You're so full of lines, Bishop. That must be your middle name."

His laughter rolled through the car. "My gun-shy, distrustful, red-haired witch."

An unexpected thrill leaped through her. The words had rolled off his lips with rough reverence. Nervous now, Maggie crossed her arms. She struggled to change to any topic other than herself. Wes was too close, and she was too responsive to him. It was a dangerous, explosive combination.

"You looked like you enjoyed getting to feel Rachel kick." Wes allowed Maggie to change the subject. He'd seen the panic in her shadowed green eyes. "That's the first time I've ever gotten to do it. It was nice of Molly to let me feel her baby kick. I don't think most women would let a stranger do that."

"Molly didn't see you as a stranger. You're my RIO, a part of our extended family, in a way. Besides, she's very perceptive with people and saw that you would enjoy the experience."

"So did you."

Maggie squirmed. What she'd enjoyed most was Wes's unexpected touch, the strength of his hand against her own. Would he be as sensitive and exploratory making love with her? She inhaled sharply and quickly looked out the window of the car to hide her reaction. Where did *that* thought come from? Wes was like a magnetic storm to the gyroscope of her heart, making her emotions spin completely out of control!

"Nothing wrong with that," Wes baited, glancing at her when she went silent on him, averting her face. Maggie's mouth was set in a line that he was beginning to realize was a defensive expression. "I like the friendship you three ladies have with one another. It's refreshing."

Relieved to be on a safer topic, Maggie said, "Molly's the Earth Mother."

"And Dana?"

"More like me, less like Molly, but she straddles the world of flying and the world of personal relationships better than I do."

"How do you see yourself in the group?"

"I'm at the extreme end—the opposite of Molly."

"Are you saying you don't ever want to get married and have children?" Wes held his breath.

Maggie squirmed in earnest now. She released a sigh and pretended to look out the side window. Of course, it was pitch-black and there was nothing out there to see. "I just see myself as the professional career-woman who carves out her niche in life."

"What about marriage?"

"I think it's a distraction of sorts. I've watched Molly's interest in flight testing wane with her being pregnant. The baby is now the center of her life, not her job."

"So, getting involved with someone would be a distraction to your career goals?"

Maggie held Wes's probing gaze. "Yes. That's why I'm not involved with anyone right now. Later, when my position is more solid and I'm not having to fight so hard for *all* women, I'll think about it.''

"Getting into a relationship doesn't always involve logic," Wes warned. "Feelings sometimes get the better of us, despite what our brain or mental processes might warn us of."

Maggie couldn't agree more. Wes Bishop was playing havoc on her feelings right now. Did he realize it? Mercilessly probing his darkened eyes, Maggie thought not.

"That's true, I guess."

"And with your red hair and Irish blood, you're certainly a woman of fierce temper and equal passion."

"There you go, using the word *passion* again!" But that was exactly what Wes evoked in her, Maggie thought—heated, longing passion for him.

He blinked. "Yeah. What's wrong with it? Italians are a very passionate people about everything... the sky, the earth, food, wine, women, children, family—"

Embarrassed and dejected, Maggie quickly responded, "Okay, okay. I took it the wrong way."

Wes grinned. He'd meant it strictly in one way to Maggie and she'd perceptively picked up on it. "It's okay, Red. You're safe with me. Remember? I'm your RIO, the guy protecting your back in a dogfight."

Later, Maggie tossed and turned in her bed. She kicked the sheet away and lay there in her shortie pajamas, staring up at the fan slowly turning above the bed. *You're safe with me.* With a groan, she flopped over on her belly and buried her head under the pillow.

"Safe," Maggie muttered to the moonlit room. "I'm about as safe with you, Bishop, as I would be with a rattlesnake in the cockpit." And it was all one-sided!

Well, that wasn't really a fair statement. Maggie sat up, threw her pillow clear across the room and crossed her legs, disgusted with her head and heart. The clock on the dresser read 0300. She had to get some sleep! But how could she, when Wes's tender expression as he felt Molly's baby kicking haunted her every time she closed her eyes? What was it about this guy that she couldn't ignore?

"You're worse than a damn cold to get rid of, Bishop!" she muttered aloud. Maggie slid off the bed and stalked toward the kitchen to make herself a cup of tea. Right now, she wished she had Molly's grandmother's recipe for an herbal tea that would put her to sleep. She'd have to call Molly tomorrow and get it.

Puttering around the kitchen, Maggie sat down at the table, completely disgruntled. What was happening to her? No man had ever affected her like this. She couldn't sleep. She couldn't stop thinking of Wes. Sipping the steaming tea, Maggie scowled. If she admitted this to either Dana or Molly, they'd take it the wrong way, clap their hands and pronounce her in love.

Was she? No, impossible! When Wes had placed his hand over hers, something terribly tender and vulnerable had broken loose within her. And it was that rampant, uncontrollable feeling which had been creating havoc in her ever since. Pushing her hair off her shoulders, Maggie sat back. Moonlight scattered through the kitchen-window curtains. When Molly had first arrived at Miramar, she'd come over and redecorated the apartment for her. Maggie had to admit the place had a much more comfortable, homey look to it now, thanks to Molly's talents.

Turning the china cup around and around on its saucer, Maggie stared down at it with a vengeance. What was this feeling that had sprung free inside her? With a sigh, Maggie decided she would have to trust her friends and speak to them about it.

It was 0900 the next morning when Maggie decided to go visit Molly in her second-floor office. Wes was out in the hangar, going over some testing routines on his instrument panel. Later, she'd join him and they'd take their daily three-hour flight.

Molly was hard at work at her desk, surrounded by paperwork when Maggie stepped in and closed the door behind her.

"Molly?"

"Hi, Maggie!"

"Got a few minutes?" Maggie sat down in a chair close to Molly's desk.

"Sure." She smiled. "Tea?"

"No, thanks. I came to talk over something with you."

"Oh?"

"Yeah." Maggie grimaced.

"Could his name be Wes Bishop?"

Maggie gave her a dirty look.

Molly laughed gently. "Oh, come on, Maggie, it's not a sin to like someone, you know."

"Bishop is my RIO. That's all."

"Do you realize that from the minute Wes arrived at my apartment, he had eyes only for you? I don't think he even tasted my meal. He was far more in touch with you sitting next to him, with what you had to say and how you interacted with all of us." Molly's smile was warm. "And the nicest, most wonderful thing was when he placed his hand over yours when you felt Rachel kicking."

"You're such a sentimental sop, Molly."

She sat up in her chair laughing. "And so are you, Maggie Donovan! You just don't know it yet. You act as if liking Wes is a terminal disease. Let's get real."

"I'm that bad, huh?"

"Yes. So, why don't you let things happen naturally between you? It's so obvious to Dana and me that you two really like each other."

"We've known each other for exactly three days, Molly."

"Time means nothing when you fall in love."

Leaping to her feet, Maggie nearly shouted, *"Love?"*

Molly winced. "Gosh, don't get so excited. You act like I shot you."

Pacing Molly's office with a vengeance, Maggie gestured wildly. "Dammit, Molly, I'm *not in love* with Bishop! This love at first sight is nothing but bull. It never happens!"

"Dana admits she fell in love with Griff at the airport the very first time she met him. And Cam told me he fell in love with me the first day he saw me coming up the walk of the test-pilot school.''

"You don't understand!" Maggie growled, throwing her hands up, pacing even more frantically. "I *don't want* to fall in love! I don't need love in my life right now! God, I've got the whole world lording over me. It's just the wrong time! The wrong place! It isn't happening. In another day or two, it'll go away and I'll be okay."

Molly sat back, her hands across her belly. "Look at you."

"Huh?" Maggie jerked to a halt. "What do you mean, look at me?"

"You're ranting and raving like a harpy eagle that got its tail feathers pulled out, Maggie. I've never seen you so upset. Other guys have liked you, but it never affected you like this."

Running her fingers across her bangs, Maggie growled, "I know it. God, I was up until 0400 this morning thinking, Molly. I can't get Bishop out of my mind. If I close my eyes, I see his face. His face, of all things! And the instant I haven't got my mind on work, I'm thinking about *him!*"

"I'd say you've fallen for the guy."

"Don't sit there looking like a Cheshire cat, Molly. You spend your life looking at the positive side of everything. You're a romantic at heart. An idealist."

"As if you don't have a little of that in your blood, too, Maggie."

"Not if I can help it. And not right *now,* Molly!"

"Come and sit down, Maggie. You look absolutely worn-out. Come on, I'll make us some tea, and we'll sit and talk about it."

Suddenly exhausted, Maggie did as Molly suggested. She dropped into the chair, shut her eyes and rubbed her brow where a headache was beginning.

"Now, if you didn't have all this awful pressure and responsibility on you, Maggie, would you be reacting the same way if Wes stepped into your life?" She handed Maggie a cup of tea and leaned against the desk to be close to her distraught friend.

"I don't know," Maggie began irritably. "I suppose not...." She took a sip of the lemony-tasting tea.

"Well, there you have it."

"Have what?"

"Your answer," Molly said with a smile.

Maggie silently eyeballed her for almost a minute. "The answer being I'm falling in love with this guy?"

"Wes isn't just any guy. I think he's wonderful."

"There you go again, Molly. You think *everyone* is wonderful!"

"Calm down. Wes is certainly unique among most of the guys we work with in the Navy. He's got some wonderful points. Look how he reacted when I let him feel Rachel kick. Did you see his eyes? His face?"

Groaning, Maggie whispered, "Don't remind me of that, Molly. That's *all* I can see!"

Leaning forward, Molly rubbed Maggie's sagging shoulder. "You poor dear. This is the first time since I've known you that you've behaved like this. I really think you are in love with Wes, and it's an entirely new experience for you. In the past, it was the guy who fell for you, not vice versa."

"It just can't be," Maggie said, her voice cracking. To her surprise, tears wedged into her eyes. Tears! Muffling a curse, she hastily wiped her eyes with the back of her hand. "I've got my career to think of! Red Flag is staring me in the face. What if I screw it up? I can't let down those girls who are dreaming about flying. Dammit, I had that same dream, and I've lived it. I want to keep that dream alive for other women. Falling in love, getting sidetracked . . . it just can't happen! It'll screw up my reflexes, my focus." And then, the truth came out in a strangled whisper. "Moll, it's one-sided. Wes doesn't like me personally. Just professionally. He treats everyone with the same kind of warmth and care. I'm not special to him."

Gently, Molly whispered Maggie's name and came over to her. She put her arm around her friend's shoulders as Maggie hung her head. "Listen to me, Maggie Donovan," she said fiercely, "I may be a cream puff in your eyes, but I've got some gray matter between my ears. I believe Wes *does* like you— personally as well as professionally." And then, more gently, she added, "You're taking your responsibilities too seriously. You've got to start easing off the throttles on them or it's going to eat you alive. My gosh, you've never failed at anything you've undertaken. Don't let Red Flag hurt you like this. The fact that you were even chosen for the team, as a woman, is enough! You don't have to win it to prove yourself."

Patting Maggie's shoulder, Molly sighed. "You've been running this race so long by yourself, Maggie. To tell you the truth, Dana and I were just waiting for this to happen. No matter how much you focus on your career, you're a human being with human needs and wants. A career doesn't replace certain things like affection, love, care, being protected and sharing laughter with someone else. The human in you has been ignored for too long, Maggie. That's why Wes Bishop has so completely unstrung you. He appeals to those secret parts within yourself that you've been ignoring."

Miserably, Maggie had to admit she couldn't refute Molly's wisdom. Molly had a skill for looking into the hearts and minds of people that Maggie had to respect. "I feel like I'm being torn in two," she admitted hoarsely. "And despite what you're saying about Wes, the people he really cares about are his ex-wife and daughter."

"I disagree with you, and time will prove I'm right, Maggie. Right now, you're torn between your career and your personal needs."

"The only choice I *can* make right now is my career, Molly. I don't have room in my life for a relationship."

"Silly, you don't *have* to make a choice," Molly said, and gave her a little shake.

Maggie lifted her chin and met Molly's dancing hazel eyes, filled with overflowing warmth. "What do you mean?"

"Because you've never been in love, you don't know how to weave it into the rest of your life, Maggie. Look at Dana: she's married, yet she's a combat pilot just like you. She's managed to weave her personal life with Griff into her professional one very successfully. And you could, too, if you wanted to.''

"Well,'' Maggie grumbled, avoiding Molly's gaze, "Dana's unique. She's got a special capability to—''

"Pooh! Dana's a human being just like you and me. There's nothing special about what she's done. I just think you need to allow certain feminine skills to surface and you can do it, too.''

"It's scary, Molly. I'm too scared to try, even if I could. Even if Wes did show he liked me more than just a little.''

Molly sighed and moved away. She walked back to her chair and sat down. "Love is always scary, Maggie. I'm scared, too. I could lose Cam. Every day I expect two officers to come walking up to tell me my husband has been lost at sea.''

Maggie groaned. "That will never happen, Molly! Cam's a good pilot.''

"You're missing my point. *Life* is scary, Maggie. Aren't you scared when you get into that cockpit with all the responsibility you carry?''

"No, not really. I just don't know what fear feels like, I guess.''

"That's highly unusual,'' Molly replied. "I've learned to live with the fear that I might lose Cam. Fear doesn't have to stop us from growing, Maggie. If it does, we stagnate or stop from fulfilling our potential as human beings—either personally or career-wise. Right now you've got fear about your feelings toward Wes. Don't run and don't hide from them. Just be yourself around him and let things develop naturally."

"I don't even know if he feels similarly about me," Maggie griped. "I mean, let's not blow this out of proportion. I've known the guy exactly three days. So what if he causes havoc in my heart? It's my craziness."

Molly smiled and ran her hand over her belly. "If I was a bettor, I'd wager every penny I own that he does like you—a lot."

Setting her empty cup on Molly's desk, Maggie got up. It was 0930 and time for her to be getting out to the hangar for a crew conference with Chantal and Wes. "You're wrong, Moll." She managed a slight smile. "Thanks for the tea and the ear. Both were good."

"See you tonight for dinner, Maggie."

As Maggie raised her hand and left, she felt curiously better but didn't understand why. Love, if that's what it really was and not just her hormones acting up, was one hell of a complex problem.

Hitching a ride in a van, Maggie thought deeply about her conversation with Molly. She was genuinely too scared to allow these feelings to develop. Everything hinged on Red Flag, and nothing must alter her focus. But why did she feel so panicky about that decision?

Chapter Six

"Oh, damn." Maggie hunted around in the cockpit of her F-14.

"What?" Wes asked from the rear seat. The heat from the late-August morning was already beginning to build, and sweat formed on his brow. He saw Maggie looking from one side of her seat to the other, hunting for something.

"My knee board. I can't find it. Where did I put it?"

Frowning, Wes said nothing. For the past month they'd been flying seven days a week, three hours a day, honing their skills for Red Flag. Things had gone smoothly, Wes supposed, on one hand. But with every day that October moved closer Maggie got more and more tense.

"Did you forget to pull it out of your duffel bag?"

"I don't know. Maybe. Some days I feel like I've lost half my brain. Where *is* that knee board?"

The knee board contained the flight sequence they would fly over the restricted area. Dana Turcotte and the two other planes representing the Navy at Red Flag were already on station, waiting for them. They would be the aggressors today while he and Maggie tried to avoid all three of them. It was going to be a tough test any way it was cut, Wes realized.

Frustration colored Maggie's command to Chantal, who stood at the base of the ladder. A special trip would have to be made back to Ops to retrieve the knee board, which would delay them a good fifteen minutes. Wes sat back, worried. In the last month, it had been hell keeping his personal feelings for Maggie aside.

"Hey, look," he said through the intercom, "don't worry about it."

"I do! Those three aircraft are flying on station burning up fuel because I can't find something as simple as a knee board."

"Red, take it easy. You're just tense about today's test. We'll beat them. Don't worry."

Maggie sat back and closed her eyes for a moment. Wes's deep voice always calmed her ragged nerves. He didn't often call her Red, but when he did, her tension seemed to melt and she felt calm again. Maggie could never explain why, but she was grateful that he used the endearment. It was so hard to keep her feelings for him under control and hidden. Molly's words haunted her, but with Red Flag only two months away,

Maggie couldn't afford to address them—or Wes. "Thanks... I just feel so stupid. It's such a rookie mistake."

"Stop being so hard on yourself. You're a human being. No one expects you to be perfect except yourself."

Maggie heard the warmth and teasing in Wes's voice. She opened her eyes and moved restlessly around the cockpit. She wanted to get this particular test out of the way. "Last week I forgot my flight maps."

"Must be getting old, lady. They say with age, memory is the first to go. Got any gray hairs?"

This time Maggie managed a short, stifled laugh. "You're good for me when I get into snits like this."

"How could I get upset with you? You want to win this test, and so do I. Just unwind up front and take it easy. We'll get your knee board and be off."

Fidgeting with various items in her cockpit, Maggie noticed how much more her hands trembled than they used to. From time to time, she'd catch Wes watching her, but he never said anything.

Exhaling forcefully, Maggie went over her array of harnesses, tightening them and doing little things to keep busy.

"If Hall hears about this, it'll be all over the base in ten minutes."

"Your ground crew isn't going to breathe a word of it, Maggie, so relax. They're proud of you and this bird you fly."

"They'll think I'm stupid."

Holding on to his patience, Wes knew what Maggie needed. Because of the mounting tension surrounding Red Flag, she was getting tunnel vision. Instead of stepping away for a day and doing something totally different, she was over-focusing on what was expected of her, and it was causing a steady decline in her ability to concentrate.

"No one thinks you're stupid, Maggie," he said gently. What she needed was to be diverted, which was a role he'd played with her since they'd become a team. "Hey, when we get off today, how about I take you over to La Jolla for a nice seafood dinner by the ocean? I found a nice, quiet restaurant over there last weekend when I was out shell hunting on the beach."

Maggie's attention was divided between watching for the dark blue van from Ops, and Wes's request. Her heart leaped and she savored the thought that this was the first time Wes had asked her out. It was impossible to ignore the heat that smoldered in his clear, intelligent blue eyes whenever he held her gaze. She always went shaky inside when that happened, and wondered if he liked her half as much as she liked him.

"I don't know...."

"It's not a date, Maggie. Just two friends going out for dinner."

Part of her was relieved. Another part was a little hurt to have it reaffirmed that he was assessing her from a professional standpoint and helping her on that level. "Well..."

"Come on, you need to get away from this place for a while. You eat, breathe and sleep Miramar. It will be a nice, quiet dinner. Okay?" Never had Wes wanted her to agree more, but he knew Maggie couldn't be pushed into anything.

It sounded heavenly to Maggie. To her relief, she saw the van coming back from Ops with her knee board. In another ten minutes, they'd be in the air. "Okay."

"Great." Wes waited for Maggie to give him grief on his response, but she didn't. This past week, she'd been concentrating so much on her job, that even her ability to tease had gotten lost. He didn't like the signs accumulating. He'd seen other pilots under similar pressure. Crashes could occur under those circumstances, and more than anything, Wes didn't want something that drastic to happen to Maggie. His sixth sense told him if disaster struck in any form before Red Flag, it could break her.

Frowning, he ruminated about that possibility. As strong as Maggie was, she was also brittle. That worried him, too. So far, her daily flying had been perfect. But small mistakes were starting to accumulate, and small mistakes had a tendency to lead to larger ones. Wes knew it took only one mistake to create an in-flight emergency. Tonight, over dinner, he told himself, he'd broach this with Maggie. Hopefully, she wouldn't get defensive about it. If she did, it would only make her more uptight than she'd already become. Damn. He walked a double-edged sword with her all the time.

"Wes?" Maggie dropped by his office, down on the first floor of Ops. He was behind his desk, up to his elbows in paperwork. When he looked up, Maggie's heart automatically took off at a gallop. How terribly handsome he was. She would never tire of looking deep into his dancing eyes.

"Yeah?" He glanced at his watch. It was almost quitting time. Maggie looked worse than when she'd come off the flight at noon today.

"Look, I'm going to beg off on that dinner with you tonight. I'm whipped. All I want to do is go home, get a hot shower and hit the sack."

Laying the pen aside, Wes nodded. "Okay. You do look tired." Maggie was pale, and subtle shadows showed beneath her glorious green eyes. Now he was genuinely worried. She stood uncertainly at his door, leaning her shoulder against the frame, her arms folded across her chest. Even now, she was defensive with him. But Wes didn't take her body language personally.

Maggie was overtired and trying to hold herself together when what she really needed was someone just to take her in his arms and hold her, Wes thought. Just hold her, without trying to make love to her. Wes knew he could give Maggie that place of safety. But at what cost to himself? Without a doubt, if he extended his care to Maggie, his heart would follow suit, and then he'd never be able to take back what was given.

Getting up, Wes walked around the desk. In a month, he'd come to admire Maggie even more. She was an incredible woman, walking a very dangerous tightrope. Lately, Wes wanted to broach Maggie's defenses despite his recently healed heart and the pain he knew his actions might cause.

Halting in front of Maggie, he followed his instincts. Her eyes were fraught with exhaustion. Wes couldn't help himself as he reached out, barely grazing her cheek with his thumb.

"Listen, it's Friday. Why don't you go home and sleep until you wake up tomorrow morning?"

Maggie was surprised by Wes's touch. Never had anything felt better to her than that glancing caress. He stood tall and strong before her, when she didn't feel much of either. "We've got an 0600 flight schedule," she said wearily. All she wanted to do was step into the circle of his arms and sink against his stalwart frame. Just for a little while.

"So, let me cancel it for us. Maggie, one day without flying isn't going to hurt our skills. A day off can often improve them."

She tucked her lower lip between her teeth, listening to his quiet, impassioned advice. "You need to rest?"

Wes saw where she was going with that question. Okay, if Maggie wouldn't admit she needed a day off, he'd play the victim. "Yeah, I'm tired, too. A day off would help me."

With a nod, she straightened, letting her arms fall to her sides. "Okay. Scratch the flight for tomorrow. Sorry I can't make dinner tonight."

"Do I get a rain check?"

She smiled tiredly. "Sure. After Red Flag?"

"I'm gone after Red Flag, remember?"

"Oh..." Upset with herself, Maggie rubbed her furrowed brow. "That's right. Sorry, I forgot."

"Hey, it's no big thing. Go home, Maggie. Sleep. I'll see you Sunday morning at 0700 here at Ops."

With a nod, she whispered, "Okay, Wes. See you then."

Genuinely worried, Wes stood in the doorway and watched Maggie walk back down the hall. Normally, she walked with a spring, her shoulders thrown back, her chin up. Lately, her proud carriage had begun to show the strain that was catching up with her.

Leaning against the door, he fixed his gaze on the black-and-white tile floor beneath his booted feet. Next week they would fly to Nellis Air Force Base, home of Red Flag, for a familiarization flight. They would spend two days acquainting themselves with the huge, sprawling base where the combat flights would take place. Almost outside the gates of Nellis was Las Vegas, Nevada. With a shake of his head, Wes meandered back into his office. Right now, Maggie was gambling for high stakes—with herself.

"Maggie, I've got a ghost on my scope bearing two-eight-five at thirteen thousand feet, the same altitude we're flying," Wes repeated with a frown. The blip on the screen disappeared, and then came back, barely visible. They were on their way to Nellis, cruising thirteen thousand feet above California's Sierra range. In another twenty minutes, they'd cross into Nevada airspace.

"A ghost? Or is it a real blip?" Maggie demanded. Sometimes the sophisticated radar on board the fighter would pick up larger birds, which appeared like ghostly objects on radar, but nothing flew at this altitude. Maggie rubbernecked around, searching the azure sky around them just in case. Below were the rugged Sierra Nevada, their peaks reaching up to over ten thousand feet, carpeted in a variety of conifers. From this altitude the mountains looked dressed in green velvet.

Eyes narrowed, Wes studied his radar, turning a dial and trying to relocate the blip. "I don't know. Maybe you ought to request a change of altitude, just in case."

"Didn't you have problems with that scope last week?"

"Yeah, it was hiccuping now and then." Wes shook his head, unable to relocate the blip. "It's probably just a ghost. I'd suggest a change in altitude."

Maggie shrugged, convinced the sky around them was clear. "Let it go," she radioed back. "Ghosts appear now and then even on the most modern of radar."

"Yeah, maybe you're right." Something bothered Wes, but he couldn't put his finger on it. He raised his head, looking around through the clear Plexiglas. The jet rumbled on, both engines paralleling the twin cockpits and sending not only sound, but a nonstop vibration through them.

"Can't be a bird you saw," Maggie added. "Eagles only fly up to ten thousand feet because of oxygen requirements. We're at thirteen. I'm sure you've just got a ghost. This is a very quiet airspace."

"You're right about the eagle." Wes watched the radar screen where the ghost had appeared with added intensity, but each sweep of the long, thin green arm revealed nothing else in that vector. Wes didn't want to push the topic. Maggie was the pilot; the ultimate decision on things like this rested in her domain.

"Might have Chantal check out that scope when we get back to Miramar, Wes."

"Roger." He knew from long experience that ghosts would show up now and then, without reason. And no matter how much maintenance or calibration was done on the delicate equipment, they tended to appear and disappear from time to time without explanation. Wes attributed it to the personality of the equipment, and in his years as an RIO, that axiom seemed to hold some truth.

Relaxing in the front seat, her right hand gently holding the stick between her legs, Maggie stopped searching the sky. Ghosts had popped up on Wes's radar before. Nothing flew at thirteen thousand, and no air traffic was in the area. They were safe.

A brown dot appeared directly ahead of the fighter. Maggie blinked. Was she seeing things? Was it an eagle? No, impossible. She opened her mouth to say something when Wes interrupted her.

"Maggie! Bogey at two-eight-zero dead ahead! Take evasive action!"

Too late! Before she could jerk the stick to the left and bank away from the golden eagle, the bird loomed huge. Flying at five hundred miles an hour, the jet closed the distance in split seconds. With a cry, Maggie threw up her gloved hand to protect her helmeted face. The bird smashed through the cockpit Plexiglas.

"Eject!" Maggie cried. "Eject! Eject!" The F-14 suddenly lagged. Bird parts were smashed all around her cockpit; the instrument panel was covered with blood, partly destroyed by the impact of the eagle. Wind pummeled Maggie, beating her, tearing at her. The buffeting increased like fists smashing into her. She wrestled with the sluggish aircraft, realizing a lot of damage had been done. Warning buzzers screamed in her ears.

Her mind worked at lightning speed. Blood smeared her visor and with her left hand, she tried to wipe enough of it away to see her instrument panel. One engine stalled. The fire-warning buzzer wailed on, joining the other screeches inside her helmet. Stopcocking the throttle, Maggie swiftly moved from one emergency to another, trying to stabilize the fighter.

Behind, she felt and heard Wes trigger the ejection seat. In seconds, he was free and clear of the ailing jet. She was going down! The fighter nosed over despite Maggie's steel grip on the stick. Jerking a look back, she saw that Wes had safely ejected. More alarms triggered. The fighter began to spiral. The altimeter unwound like a broken spring, and the F-14's nose pointed straight down toward the green mountains.

With a cry, Maggie tried with everything she could to pull the fighter out of the spin. The G's built up in a hurry, pinning her against the seat. She was barely able to move her hand. She couldn't lose this plane! She just couldn't!

At six thousand feet, Maggie had to give up. She jerked the handles beneath her ejection seat, bailing out. The rockets fired. Eyes closed, she felt the chair jerk free of the crippled fighter. She'd lost a fighter! Oh, God, she'd never be able to live it down! What would they do to her? What would happen? And Wes! Had Wes made a safe landing? A million thoughts crowded into Maggie's mind as her parachute snaked out.

The nylon chute billowed open. She went from the roaring noises of the cockpit to cold, dead silence. Looking around, Maggie tried to spot her fighter. She saw the F-14 nosing over on its back, arcing down between two huge mountains a good ten or twenty miles away from where she swung in the sky. Twisting around, Maggie searched frantically for Wes. She was alone in the sky, the only chute visible. Her terror turned to anguish.

Tears leaked into Maggie's eyes. The distant crash of the jet could be heard in a series of thunderous, rolling booms. She was too far away to feel its reverberations, the jet having disappeared into some valley miles to the south of her. The earth was coming up fast now. Maggie sobbed, pulling on the risers to help guide her down. If she landed in the conifers that seemed to jut up toward her like green spears, she could be killed on impact herself.

Spotting a long, rolling meadow just below the ten thousand-foot level of a huge, granite mountain, Maggie focused her dazed mind on trying to land there, instead. The wind was gentle, so the chute responded well to her guidance via the risers. The flat, rolling expanse of the meadow drew closer. Maggie tried to remember everything she'd been taught about bailouts. She kept her feet together, her knees slightly bent and flexed to take the fall. *Roll.* She had to roll, or she could break an ankle or a leg.

The earth came up fast. Taking a ragged breath, Maggie closed her eyes just before hitting the earth. Her feet struck the grass, and she flexed, forcing herself to keep her body as relaxed as possible, and rolled. The shock was evenly distributed, and when Maggie stopped rolling, she lay spread-eagled on her back, looking up at the dark blue sky through her helmet visor, still streaked with blood.

The wind was knocked out of her, and she lay still for a good minute, gasping for air. The nylon chute had trailed behind her, a long white ribbon flowing across the meadow. Rolling onto her side with a groan, Maggie slowly got to her knees. With shaking hands, she began to unsnap the array of harnesses. They dropped one by one around her. Last to come off was her helmet. She stared at it. The helmet had been badly damaged. She was lucky not to have been knocked unconscious by the collision. If she had been, she'd have gone down with the fighter.

Grimacing, Maggie dropped the helmet, not wanting to look at it too closely. What about Wes? In shock, Maggie knelt, torn between concern for his status and checking herself for injury. Did she have any broken bones? Moving her arms and legs, she determined there were none. When she got to her feet, she staggered but caught herself. Her back ached as if it were on fire; one ankle was tender. Otherwise, Maggie knew she'd survived.

Standing alone in the middle of the quiet, sun-bathed meadow, Maggie choked back a sob. Where was Wes? He'd bailed out, but where was he? Had his chute opened after ejection? She should have seen his chute after she'd bailed out, but hadn't. Taking off her Nomex gloves, Maggie felt her world shattering around her, and she slumped back to her knees, tears blurring her vision. Had she lost her RIO plus the plane? Maggie couldn't live with that. Wes *had* to be alive! He just had to be!

Alone in the meadow, deep in shock, Maggie did nothing for the next hour. Her mind refused to function. Her emotions were a quagmire of anguish, grief and fear. Finally, her mind began to work again. By now, the sun was hanging in the western part of the sky. Checking her wristwatch, Maggie saw it was 1400.

She looked up and searched the meadow. Where was Wes? God, he couldn't be dead! Maggie got to her feet, a little steadier now. Her hair had come unbound and flowed around the shoulders of her flight suit. She had to think. She had to plan. Where was she? In which direction would Wes have landed? Maggie refused to see him dead.

So many details tugged at her. As she took stock of the situation, Maggie knew that she hadn't had the time to issue a Mayday distress call that any nearby military or civilian airport would pick up and report to the FAA. No one knew they'd crashed, unless a forest-service lookout had seen the F-14 go down. Even then, the fighter was so far south that rescue teams would never find them here.

Moving to her harness and equipment, Maggie checked the small radio attached to one of the straps. It could emit a Mayday signal and possibly help them be picked up. Leaning down, however, she saw that the radio had been smashed—probably by the eagle exploding through the Plexiglas canopy.

Shakily, Maggie took the small bit of food supplied and stored it in the many pockets of her baggy flight suit. The emergency kit wouldn't leave her totally abandoned, and having taken a survival course years before, Maggie knew she could subsist on food around her for a long time, if necessary.

First, she had to try to locate Wes. Picking up the knife in its leather sheath, she tried to concentrate on directions. Though she stood in blazing sunlight, Maggie shivered; the wind was cool at this altitude on the mountain. Her heart burst with such anguish and overwhelming emotion that all she could do was sob. On the heels of it came the realization that she loved Wes. Oh, God, why had she ignored how she felt about him? What if he was dead? What about Annie, the daughter he loved so fiercely?

"No!" Maggie rasped angrily. "No, dammit. He's not dead!" And she tramped off, heading in a southerly direction, leaving the meadow behind. She refused to acknowledge that Wes's chute might not have opened. One way or another, Maggie would locate him. He had to be alive! He just had to be!

Molly's fateful words ran around in her head as she walked mile after mile down the rock-laden slope, weaving in and around the pine trees. The forest surface was slippery with dried pine needles, and more than once, Maggie fell. She didn't care, brutally pushing her already bruised body to its limits. At this altitude, even though she was in superb physical shape, Maggie was gasping for air.

At least once an hour, Maggie would halt and rest for ten minutes—just long enough to catch her breath. Her mind whirled with pain and grief. Tears kept leaking into her eyes and down her drawn cheeks. Maggie felt totally bereft and disoriented. Only the compass in her hand told her she was still continuing north. Where was Wes? Maggie needed him. She'd never needed anyone in all her life, but right now she'd have traded everything she'd ever owned or accomplished just to be held in the safety of Wes's embrace.

Molly's words whispered back to her, haunting her, and she couldn't get them to stop replaying in her head. Okay, she loved Wes. But it was too late. Too late! What was really important? As Maggie trudged down the slope, her mind and emotions mired in shock, she no longer knew the answer to that. Her brilliant career had come to an abrupt end with this crash and the loss of a thirty-five-million-dollar aircraft. Worse, she'd ignored her love for Wes and opted for her career. Now, what did she have left? Nothing.

At the base of the forest-covered mountain, Maggie halted. In front of her was another mountain to climb. She stood still, wavering unsteadily on her feet, her vision blurred with tears. As never before, she saw her life in perspective: that of a woman driven by demon powers to succeed at any cost to herself—even at the cost of love, of being loved and having a life outside the cockpit. Hadn't Wes gently treaded that ground with her early on in their relationship?

Miserable, Maggie wiped her eyes with the back of her bruised and cut hand. As she stood in the cathedral-like silence of the forest, the colors and the life that throbbed within it struck Maggie for the first time. Before, from her lofty position in the jet, it had been nothing more than an expanse of green below her. How much had she cut herself off from life? From experiencing other sights, sounds, colors and textures?

Maggie hurt so much that she sank to the ground, covered her face with both hands and sobbed in earnest. She was alone. Completely alone. No one knew where she was. Did anyone care? Probably not. She'd built herself an ivory tower where friendship, other than with Dana and Molly, had no chance to grow. Worst of all, she'd spurned Wes Bishop. Sitting there, Maggie wondered if in his own quiet, subtle way, Wes had been telling her all along that he really liked her and wanted the right to get to know her better. Just last week, she'd turned down dinner with him. God, she'd been so selfish at the expense of everyone around her. And worse, she couldn't be sure if he honestly liked her. At least now, she admitted her love for him.

Her sobs were loud and without apology, the sound swallowed up by the forest around her. Maggie didn't care, and her weeping turned more into the howl of a wounded wolf without a mate. Another sound barely impinged on her consciousness, so caught up was she in her pain and her tears. Then, she distinctly heard her name called.

Lifting her chin, Maggie looked in the direction of the voice. Her eyes wet with tears, she could barely make out the form of a man descending the slope of the other mountain and coming in her direction.

"Wes?" she whispered, staggering to her feet. "Wes? Is that you?" For a terrible instant, Maggie wondered if she'd gone off the deep end, imagining the whole thing. As the form drew closer, Maggie wiped the tears from her eyes and was able to see him clearly.

"Wes!" she cried, her voice cracking.

Chapter Seven

Maggie's cry shattered the stillness. It was like a knife serrating Wes's heart, his soul. Even in the dusky light, with the gloom settling upon the forest around them, Wes could clearly see the toll the crash had taken on Maggie. He trotted down the steep, rocky slope toward her. As he neared, his heart began to hammer in earnest.

Maggie limped toward him, her eyes red from crying. She looked like a bedraggled ragamuffin, her flight suit torn in several places, her hands scratched and bloodied from the ejection. That mass of red hair, with pine needles caught in its strands, was in dire need of a brushing. There was a huge cut on her brow, probably caused by the eagle.

As Wes closed the distance to where Maggie staggered toward him, he realized she could have died. And suddenly, nothing mattered except that he loved her. No longer would he try to avoid that fact. When he looked into her dazed eyes, Wes grew more worried about Maggie's mental state. It was obvious she was in shock.

"Come here," he rasped, dragging Maggie into his arms. He pulled her against him and held her so tightly he was afraid he'd hurt her. "God! I thought I'd lost you, Maggie."

Maggie sagged against the safety of Wes's bulk. Her hands went around his waist, and she pressed her cheek against his uniform, her eyes tightly shut.

"I—I thought you died in the crash," she sobbed. "I didn't see a chute after I ejected. I was so afraid... afraid, Wes..."

"Shh, it's okay, Red. I'm here and I'm okay." He pressed a series of kisses to her thick, abundant hair. Inhaling her fragrance, he could also smell the familiar odor of fear mingled with sweat on her uniform. They'd both had a close call. Groaning when Maggie buried her head deeply in his shoulder, he smiled.

"This is right. God, it's so right. Go ahead. Just rest, Maggie. You're so tired. I'll hold you...." He pressed a kiss to her temple. The need to kiss her lips was excruciating, but Wes controlled that wild desire. She was breathing raggedly against him, holding him as tightly as she could. She reminded him of a child who'd had a terrible nightmare, turning to him for protection and comfort.

Those were things Wes could give her. He tried to separate his own growing love for Maggie from how she received his embrace. To her, it probably wasn't love at all. She was clinging to him, as she would to anyone in the same circumstances. It was only natural. And it didn't matter if his love for her was one-sided.

Gently he eased her back enough to study her more closely. In the gray light of dusk, he saw the utter devastation in her eyes that the crash had caused. Her lower lip trembled, and he caressed her scratched and dirtied cheek.

"It's all right, honey. We're both safe. Come on, let's sit down. It's almost dark, and rescue isn't coming tonight."

Woodenly, Maggie allowed Wes to guide her to the trunk of a huge pine tree. When he sat down with his back against it, he drew her into the fold of his embrace. Tiredly she lay against him, content to feel his arms go around her once more.

"Better?" Wes murmured against her ear. How warm and soft Maggie felt against him. She was trembling. Violently, now. Crooning softly to her, he held and rocked her. Darkness stole swiftly and silently over them, yet, strangely, Wes had never felt more content than he did right now. He knew Maggie was having a letdown after the crash and was starting to come out of shock. Taking his hand, he stroked her hair, shoulders and back, giving her the safe place she needed. Very soon her trembling abated, and she clung to him, her face pressed into his shoulder.

Later, as Wes lay with Maggie sleeping in his arms, with dried pine needles for a bed, he watched the stars grow bright and near in the patches of ebony sky between the branches of the conifers. Because it was the hottest part of the summer, even at this altitude it wasn't really cold. Chilly, yes, but with Maggie next to him, Wes was warm. In a way, just having Maggie close helped him ease out of his own shock from the ejection. His mind gradually cleared as the night wore on, and sometime—around midnight, Wes estimated—he, too, fell asleep. Only this time, the woman he loved with a fierceness he'd never thought possible, slept in his arms. It was something Wes had never dared hope would happen; but dreams had a way of coming true, his idealistic heart whispered to him as he surrendered to exhaustion.

The cheery tune of a brilliant red cardinal sitting on a branch in the pine tree opposite from where Wes slept, awoke him. Drowsily he barely opened his eyes and focused on Maggie. She slept deeply against him, her breathing slow and even. Her hand lay on his chest, close to her face; the mass of her hair was like a scarlet coverlet emphasizing her clean, honest beauty.

Wes sighed, crazily feeling happier than he could ever recall. The cardinal kept singing, and it was like a song urging the pale pink dawn to break around them. Lifting his hand, he idly picked out the pine needles that had become entangled in Maggie's long hair. The ends were curled, but the rest of her hair was a shining sheet across her shoulder, arm and his chest. What would it be like to wake up after making love with Maggie, to have her flowing red strands spread across his chest like fire?

The thought tormented Wes. Gently he grazed her dusty cheek, feeling the pliancy of her flesh beneath his thumb. Her lips, lush and ripe, were parted as if begging to be tasted by his mouth. What would it be like to kiss her? Would she be as hot and fiery as that hair of hers promised? Tentative? Maybe even a little shy? Wes lay there a good five minutes pondering each of those possibilities and liking all of them.

Gradually his mind cleared of sleep and he blinked, forcing himself to wake up completely. Maggie, seeming to sense that he wanted to get up and move about, stirred fitfully in his arms. His gaze never left her face, and he absorbed her awakening like a man starved for something he'd never taste again. Her red lashes were long and thick, like her hair. They fluttered against the dark shadows beneath her eyes. As Maggie started to move, she groaned. Automatically, Wes tightened his grip around her.

"Take it easy, Red. You're going to be sore as hell from that ejection," he whispered. How easy it would be to lean those few inches to cover her mouth with his. Wes groaned—not because he was stiff and sore, but because he could barely stand the tension of not kissing her.

Maggie felt and heard Wes groan. She inhaled deeply, realizing she'd slept in his arms all night. Never had anything felt so good to her. Not even flying. That tiny revelation clung to her just-awakening senses as she forced her lashes open. The dawn was a pale pink through the hundreds of pine trees that covered the slope where they lay. The gentle strength of Wes's arms about her soothed the ragged edges of her emotions. He gave her a sense of calm when now, more fully conscious, she realized that as beautiful as the world appeared this morning, her life was in shattered pieces around her.

"How do you feel?" Wes asked, helping Maggie to sit up. She put a hand against her cut forehead.

"Like hell," she murmured. "Even talking hurts."

Slowly getting to his knees, Wes unzipped a leg pocket in his flight suit and drew out a first-aid kit. "Let me clean and bandage that for you." He found a tin of aspirins. Claiming one of her hands, he placed two tablets in it. "Take these."

Wrinkling her nose, she stared at them. "Without water?"

"Afraid so, honey."

A warmth enveloped Maggie at his apologetic tone. Despite the size of Wes's hands, he was excruciatingly gentle in cleaning her sizable cut. Maggie sat very still, letting the aspirins melt at the back of her mouth. She tried not to wince when he applied the antiseptic to the wound.

"It's got to hurt," he murmured. Her eyes were narrowed with pain, her lips compressed, but she said nothing. "Head wounds always bleed like stuck hogs," he commented after applying a clean white gauze dressing to the cut. Wes patiently cleaned off the side of Maggie's face and neck where blood had dried.

Maggie sat, eyes closed, absorbing his touch, needing it badly. Amazed that the pain seemed almost gone after he'd dressed the cut, Maggie said nothing. Wes was healing to her. This was something Maggie had become starkly aware of during the past month. Just the calm assurance of his voice could ease some of the terrible tension that stalked her before each combat flight.

"Thanks, Wes."

He sat down and replaced all the items in the plastic first-aid kit. "You're welcome." Worried, he studied her profile. "Time for assessment. How are you doing?"

She refused to meet his eyes. "How would you feel after losing a thirty-five-million-dollar aircraft? I'm washed up. My career's down the tubes." Her voice cracked. "Worst of all, I've failed not only myself, but all those other women."

How fragile Maggie was. Wes had almost said it. He reached out, resting his hand against her slumped shoulder. "Now, listen to me—this crash wasn't your fault, Maggie. Once the board of inquiry hears our story, we'll both be cleared."

She barely turned her head. "If I were a male pilot, that might be true. But a woman was flying the plane, and in charge. No, they'll blow this out of proportion. The news media will jump on it and I'll be a scapegoat whether I deserve it or not." The darkness of Wes's beard made him look twice as dangerous to her as before. It also compounded how handsome he was. He looked fine despite the ejection; not a scratch on him. For that, she was grateful.

Wes ached to take Maggie into his arms. Her eyes still showed how devastating the flight accident had been for her. Where once there had been a sparkle of defiance, there was instead the gloom of defeat. Where once he'd seen the gold of hope, he saw the depths of desolation. "Don't do this to yourself, Maggie. Yeah, the news media might play it for all it's worth, but I don't think the board is going to gut you."

She shook her head, feeling tears rush into her eyes. Turning away from Wes because she didn't want him to see her cry, she croaked, "I've failed, Wes! I failed! I blew it."

"That's enough," he whispered tautly, gripping her by the arms and forcing her to look at him. The shock value of his action registered on her pale, drawn features. "Stop feeling sorry for yourself and start looking at the positives, will you? We're both alive, thank God. We've got some aches, pains, bruises and cuts, but basically, we're in good shape. I've seen guys killed by ejecting." He gave her a gentle shake. The pain in Maggie's eyes nearly unstrung him. She was genuinely depressed in a way he'd never seen before. "First things first, Maggie. We've got to get rescued. Let's do this a day at a time. We'll worry about the board after we're picked up."

All Maggie wanted to do was to fall into Wes's arms and cry. Valiantly she fought back the tears, wildly aware of his hands on her arms. "Okay..."

Sliding his hands down her arms, Wes captured her hands, which were laced with small scratches. "You're in worse shape than I am. How about if I start making some command decisions for us?"

She nodded. "Yeah ... fine."

"Good." Wes wanted to convince her that everything was going to be all right, but his words didn't

You may be the winner of the

MILLION DOLLAR
GRAND PRIZE!

$1,000,000.00	**MILLION**	$1,000,000.00
DOLLAR GRAND PRIZE		
SWEEPSTAKES ENTRY STICKER		
$1,000,000.00		$1,000,000.00

| OVER EIGHT THOUSAND OTHER PRIZES | WIN A MUSTANG BONUS PRIZE | WIN THE ALOHA HAWAII VACATION BONUS PRIZE |
| Guaranteed **FOUR FREE BOOKS** No obligation to buy! | Guaranteed FREE VICTORIAN PICTURE FRAME No cost! | Guaranteed **PLUS A MYSTERY GIFT** Absolutely free! |

ENTER SILHOUETTE'S BIGGEST SWEEPSTAKES EVER!

This lovely Victorian pewter-finish miniature is perfect for displaying a treasured photograph. And it's yours FREE as added thanks for giving our Reader Service a try!

Silhouette Reader Service™ Sweepstakes Entry Form

This is your **unique** Sweepstakes Entry Number: 2B 122843

> This could be your lucky day! If you have the winning number, you could be the Grand Prize Winner. To be eligible, *affix Sweepstakes Entry Sticker here!* **(SEE RULES IN BACK OF BOOK FOR DETAILS)**

> If you would like a chance to win the $25,000.00 prize, the $10,000.00 prize, or one of many $5,000.00, $1,000.00, $250.00 or $10.00 prizes... plus the Mustang and the Hawaiian Vacation, *affix Bonus Prize Sticker here!*

> To receive free books and gifts with no obligation to buy, as explained on the opposite page, *affix the Free Books and Gifts Sticker here!*

Please enter me in the sweepstakes and, when the winner is drawn, tell me if I've won the $1,000,000.00 Grand Prize! Also tell me if I've won any other prize, including the car and the vacation prize. Please ship me the free books and gifts I've requested with sticker above. Entering the Sweepstakes costs me nothing and places me under no obligation to buy! (If you do not wish to receive free books and gifts, do not affix the FREE BOOKS AND GIFTS sticker.)

235 CIS ACL3

YOUR NAME	PLEASE PRINT	
ADDRESS		APT#
CITY	STATE	ZIP

Silhouette "No Risk" Guarantee

- You're not required to buy a single book—ever!
- As a subscriber, you must be completely satisfied or you may cancel at any time by marking "cancel" on your statement or by returning a shipment of books at our cost.
- The free books and gifts you receive are yours to keep.

ALTERNATE MEANS OF ENTRY: Print your name and address on a 3" x 5" piece of plain paper and send to: Silhouette's Wishbook Sweepstakes, 3010 Walden Ave., P.O. Box 1867, Buffalo, N.Y. 14269-1867 seem to affect her. Maggie was in some kind of internal, emotional tailspin, and it had Wes stymied. He'd seen guys go into depression after a bailout, but not to this degree of despondency. Maybe, in the hours ahead as they found their way out of the Sierra Nevada, he might be able to figure why she was behaving this way.

"According to my navigation map, there was a small town we flew over just before the emergency. It's called Grayeagle, and it's just inside the California border." He turned, studying the mountains that rose on all sides of them. "If we can make it there, we can call Miramar for Rescue to come and pick us up."

"I think it's the only way." Maggie's mouth twisted. "My radio was damaged. How about yours?"

"It works, but only for a five-mile radius, which isn't much. That bird of ours flew a hell of a long way before augering in, and I know if it was picked up by the fire lookouts of the forest service, the Navy will concentrate their rescue efforts over there, first, and miss us completely in their search pattern."

"And by that time, we could be in Grayeagle," Maggie guessed.

"If my memory serves me correctly, we're probably fifty miles east of Grayeagle. That's an easy two-day walk."

"Your plan's a good one."

Wes dug into the other pant-leg pocket of his flight suit. "I've got even better news: we'll eat well. Take a look."

Maggie watched as he drew out ten candy bars and at least ten small packages of salted nuts. He was grinning like a little boy. "Your junk food."

"Don't sound so disgusted, Red. I know you don't eat this stuff, but there's no choice now. And don't give it such a dirty look. It's better than killing a snake or eating bugs the way survival school taught us."

Maggie tried to rally to his teasing, but it was just impossible under the circumstances. Slowly, she got to her feet. Her back felt cranky and stiff. "We'd better get going, then," she said quietly.

Stuffing their food supply back into the pocket, Wes got up and put his hand around her upper arm. "Let's go for it, Donovan."

The day was perfect, Maggie thought, as they walked, the miles unwinding before them. But she couldn't enjoy the colors, the smell of pine, the melodic calls of the birds or anything else. Emotionally, she was numb. The only thing that gave her any feeling, any hope at all, was Wes walking at her side. For the first hour, he kept his hand on her arm, as if afraid she would get dizzy or fall. She did neither, and later he released her, but he always remained mere inches away. His closeness gave her stability.

Near noon, down in a valley, Wes spotted a small stream. Maggie was looking pale, so he led her over to the rocky creek flowing with pure, clear water, and made her sit down. She just wasn't herself in any way, shape or form. Normally, if there was a hair out of place, she'd be taming it back with her fingers. Her thick hair was an unruly tangle, yet she appeared not to care.

Maggie leaned over the stream, cupped her hands and drank thirstily. Wes joined her, slurping noisily at her side. Afterward, Maggie scrubbed her face, neck and arms with moss growing along the bank. She longed for a hot tub of water, but this would have to do. Wes followed suit, only he stripped to the waist.

As Maggie sat on the grassy bank, the sun stealing in to make light-and-dark patterns through the tree branches around her, Maggie watched Wes wash. Normally, Navy personnel all wore cotton T-shirts beneath their flight suits, but he didn't. He'd hitched up the long sleeves of his suit and tied them about his waist so it wouldn't fall to his feet. She wondered if he wore briefs or boxer shorts. Wes seemed totally unconcerned about his nakedness, and scrubbed himself vigorously with the scratchy green moss.

His chest was broad and deep, with a carpet of thick, black hair across it, and Maggie thought he was beautiful in a way only a man could be. But her senses were skewed from the crash, and although Wes was a feast for her eyes, she simply couldn't appreciate him as she normally might. Still, the fact that he was here, with her, gave her some semblance of security.

Sitting back down on the bank to let the sunlight and breeze dry his upper body, Wes smiled over at her. "Too bad you can't do the same thing," he teased. When Maggie didn't respond, Wes added, "Of course, I could turn my back and you could undress and wash here if you wanted. I wouldn't look."

The faraway look in Maggie's eyes bothered him. Frowning, Wes dug into his pant-leg pocket and produced a pack of peanuts. "Here, Maggie. I want you to eat these."

She stared at his hand and the peanuts.

"Maggie?"

"Yes?"

A part of him wanted to shake her. What the hell was happening to her? "Are you all right? Is that cut on your head bothering you?"

"The cut?" She saw the concern burning in his eyes. "Oh . . . the cut. No, it's fine. My headache's gone."

Maybe Maggie was still in shock. She certainly was acting as if she were. Patiently, Wes put the peanuts into her hand. "I want you to eat these."

"I'm not really hungry, Wes."

The old Maggie was gone, and that frightened him. She was behaving like a robot, devoid of emotion. "I don't care. You need to eat."

Maggie ate the food but didn't taste it. Then she lay down on the springy carpet of grass, using her hands as a pillow for her head. In no time, she was asleep.

Wes sat on the sunny bank, munching a candy bar while Maggie slept. Maybe she was just exhausted, he reassured himself. His protective side was working overtime with her. The sunlight and shadow danced across her long, slender form. He watched the light caress her red hair, picking out highlights. The darkness beneath her eyes had increased.

Getting to his feet, Wes shrugged back into his flight suit and zipped it up. By his estimation, they'd traveled fifteen to eighteen miles this morning. If Maggie was up to it, they'd go twenty more this afternoon. He was sure that by the time night fell, they'd both be exhausted. Whatever was wrong with Maggie had to be treated by a doctor. And the sooner he got her to one, the better.

* * *

"Let's call a halt," Wes ordered, holding out his hand when Maggie stumbled slightly. He gripped her by the arm and gently swung her around. Dusk was giving way to night, and they had to find a place to stay. When Maggie came without hesitation into his arms, Wes groaned.

"This is heaven," he rasped, holding her tightly, feeling the curves of her fit against his tall frame. "You're heaven, Maggie."

The whisper of his breath across her cheek gave Maggie sustenance. When she felt his mouth on her temple in a kiss, she sighed.

"I'm so glad you're here with me, Wes. I wouldn't know what to do without you...."

The quaver in her voice tore at him. He smiled against her temple; the strands of her hair felt silky beneath his mouth. "Yes, you would, Red. You're too strong and self-reliant not to be."

"Not right now," Maggie whispered, and raised her chin to meet his hooded stare. Everything had been numb within her until just a few hours ago. Maggie was beginning to feel again. Wes's smoldering blue eyes made her heart take wing, and she felt an incredible desire to kiss him. She needed Wes. She needed what he was silently offering her in the form of his embrace and what she saw so clearly written in his eyes.

It was the most natural thing in the world, Wes realized as he leaned down to capture her offering. He'd wondered and worried if Maggie would ever want to kiss him the way he wanted to kiss her. Now, as she

stood in the circle of his arms, with her head lifted and
a bit of life returning to her lovely green eyes, he read
her need. As his mouth fitted perfectly over hers, a
deep, searing heat tore loose within him. She tasted of
pine, the salt of perspiration, and sweet chocolate. Her
breath was moist and ragged against his face as he
deepened his exploration of her. There was such
sweetness, such boldness coupled with vulnerability in
her as she returned his kiss.

Maggie's world drew to a halt; all her reawakening
senses focused on Wes. His mouth was powerful and
hungry against hers, and she drank of the strength he
was sharing with her. As his tongue traced each corner of her mouth, then tasted her lower lip, she trembled violently in his arms. Automatically he held her
more tightly, feeling her breasts pressed to his chest
and the thudding beat of his heart synchronizing with
her own.

Day and night melted together as Maggie closed her
eyes and slid her arms around his broad and so-very-
capable shoulders. A deep, primal urge to make love
with him startled her. It was a need like no other she'd
ever experienced. As she hungrily returned his kiss,
threading her fingers through the thick hair at the nape
of his neck, Maggie had never wanted anything more.
Unconsciously, she pressed her hips against his.

Wes groaned, sliding his hand down her long,
deeply curved back and capturing her hips. Dizzied by
Maggie's sudden desire blossoming from their searing kiss, he tried to control his own explosive hunger.
A part of his mind screamed at him that she was acting this way because she'd nearly died. It was a well-

known fact that after a near-death experience, people frequently needed to make love in order to feel alive. Disheartened, Wes gently but firmly eased his mouth from her wet, enticing lips. Maggie's eyes were dazed with a passion as fierce as the heat that throbbed through his own hard, ready body.

"Come on, Red, we've got to rest. We're both still in shock." His words were whispered hoarsely. They barely impinged on Maggie as she stood looking up at him. Wes knew that if he made love to her now, he'd hate himself later. "This isn't the time or place, Maggie. Do you understand that?"

Disappointed and needing to drown herself in his arms, his mouth and his body, Maggie sighed. The terrible, devastating realization that Wes had kissed her because she wanted it, avalanched through her. She'd been right all along: her love was one-sided. "Okay, I'll trust your judgment. Mine's gone to hell."

Wes managed a sour grin. Some of the old Maggie was returning. He gave her a swift kiss on her lips. "At least we can hold each other while we sleep. That's not such a bad trade-off, is it?"

She knelt down where he indicated. A huge tree, three times the girth of any man, had been struck by lightning and gutted out many years before. What was left after the strike was a carved-out six-foot-tall stump. It would provide them a perfect shelter. Maggie crawled inside; the wood surrounded her on three sides. Wes followed and promptly lay down. He patted his arm as he stretched out.

"Here's the best pillow in town."

Maggie got to her knees and lay down with her back to him. When she rested her head on his upper arm, she felt Wes change position and move onto his side, placing his other arm around her waist.

"Better?" he asked, his face nestled in her hair on her shoulder.

"Much better," Maggie admitted tiredly while her heart cried with grief. Wes didn't love her. Never had. And she loved him with such fierceness and passion that it was ruling her life in all spheres.

"We'll stay warm this way."

"Okay," she whispered. Somewhere in her fogged brain and injured heart, Maggie knew she was going to savor every second in Wes's arms. It would have to last her a lifetime.

The old Maggie would have given him grief for that lame line of his. Wes kept his worry to himself, though. Bringing her fully against his body, he whispered, "Go to sleep, Red. Tomorrow's a better day. We can't be more than ten miles from Grayeagle, and then we'll call for rescue. Good night."

Her lashes had already drooped closed. Maggie savored his closeness, his hope when she had lost hers. "Good night, Wes. And thanks—for everything."

He raised his head and kissed her cheek. "Go to sleep, honey. You'll feel better in the morning."

As much as Maggie wanted to go to sleep, her mind and emotions refused to shut down. Wildly aware of Wes's masculine length outlining her own, the ache in her only intensified. An unexpected desperation within her wanted to make wild, primal love with him. The woman in her needed the man in him. It was that simple and that complex. Maggie's mind, however, was on a completely different tangent: the board-of-inquiry investigation of her crash. Would they find her guilty of flight negligence? Suspend her? Take her off Red Flag?

The only constancy and stability Maggie felt was being in Wes's arms, his soft, occasional snore close to her ear, his moist breath caressing her cheek. For hours on end, Maggie replayed the crash and her efforts to prevent it, trying to second-guess what a board of her superiors might think. Sometime during the night, Maggie slept. Once, near dawn, she woke up. She had turned over; her face was snuggled in the crook of Wes's shoulder, her body solidly against his. There was such peace in his arms, while all around her, her world was falling apart.

Chapter Eight

Maggie broke out in a cold sweat when two Navy commanders from the board of inquiry approached them at Ops after they'd arrived at Miramar the next day. Night had already fallen when they were ordered into separate debrief rooms to make out individual reports on the crash.

Although her back was sore, sick bay had earlier pronounced her fit to fly again, once the psychiatric evaluation and interview were conducted. And so was Wes. She gave him a panicked look before she went into the small cubicle to fill out her report. Wes offered a slight smile meant to silently buoy her flagging spirits.

Sitting alone after receiving instructions on how to fill out the long and involved report, Maggie glanced at her wristwatch. It was 2200 and she was exhausted. Once they'd reached Grayeagle that morning, the Navy had sent a Shore Patrol vehicle to retrieve them. From there, they'd taken a flight out of Sacramento and had arrived at Miramar by noon.

Rubbing her head, which still hurt from the injury, Maggie sat with her elbows on the table, her eyes closed. The report she had to write—the one her entire career hinged on—could wait a few more minutes. Everything had been rushed since they'd set foot back on Miramar. Reporters had hounded them, although the Navy didn't allow them to talk to Maggie and Wes. Maggie wondered what kind of press *she* was getting. She'd been the pilot in charge. It was her neck on the line.

Sighing, Maggie picked up the pen. She'd been through an extensive physical at sick bay early that afternoon. Then she'd had a long session with the psychiatrist, who sat behind his desk and black-rimmed glasses, saying little but writing a lot on the paper before him. Was she fit to fly again? He would tell her shortly. Any pilot who ejected went through these procedures. They were a pain in the rear.

Lifting her head, Maggie opened her eyes and stared at the light blue wall. If it hadn't been for Dana and Molly meeting her shortly after she and Wes had returned, Maggie would have felt completely abandoned. Naturally, they'd heard about the crash; it was their warmth and joy at seeing her alive that gave Maggie some semblance of hope.

Get with it, Donovan—they aren't going to let you out of here until they've got your report in hand,

Maggie chided herself. She had to think. Clearly. Everything she put on the report would have a bearing on the determination of the board of inquiry as to whether she'd be charged with negligence, or cleared. It seemed almost impossible to think. Her heart lingered over the fact that after they were picked up in Grayeagle, Wes's touches, his arm around her shoulder and husky words of encouragement had ended. Abruptly. Now he was all business—back to his old self, she supposed. How desperately Maggie missed his tender care of her during their two-day trek out of the forest.

Maggie couldn't get the worry of her boss, Commander Parkinson, out of her mind, either. He'd been solicitous, asking personal questions about how she was feeling—unlike the other board officers, who glared at her, silently accusing her of destroying a thirty-five-million-dollar plane owned by the taxpayers. Yet no one felt worse than Maggie did. No one.

Her hand shook badly as she tried to print clearly on the paper. Ink smudged the report. With a muffled sound, Maggie sat back, tears welling up into her eyes. Tears! She rarely cried, but since the crash, that was all she seemed able to do.

For no particular reason, Maggie wanted Wes with her. She fantasized that he would hold her, say the right things and help her get her strewn emotions back into a semblance of order. It was all an impossible dream. Wes's concern after the crash had been to help her professionally, not personally. Wiping her eyes, she was thankful that no one saw her crying. It would only work against her in this men's Navy.

Wes. A little sigh escaped Maggie as she doggedly wrote on. Mixed in with her fear of losing her career and being discharged were her feelings for him—wild, throbbing feelings as bright as hot sunlight, filled with hope, and seeming to breathe life into her. What had happened? Was it the molten kiss they'd shared in the mountains? Or was it the moment he'd discovered her after the crash and pulled her into his strong, protective arms?

Whatever it was, Maggie reflected tiredly, finally signing her name to the report, it was good and positive. Just thinking about Wes soothed her. Rubbing her smarting, burning eyes, Maggie slowly got to her feet. She ached inside and out, wanting only a hot shower and then bed.

As she opened the door, the Shore Patrol sentry at the door came to attention. Maggie didn't like the idea they were being guarded, but the press had their own sneaky ways of trying to ferret out the unlucky individual who was in their gun sights for an interview. It was a necessary precaution.

"Take this to Commander Williams," she told the guard. Down the hall, she noticed Wes standing talking with his sentry. Was he waiting for her? Gratitude filled Maggie as she realized that was exactly what Wes was doing. She walked down the long, deserted hall toward him.

Unaccountably, Maggie's heart lifted and so did her beaten spirit. In her opinion, Wes looked far better for the experience than she felt. As she approached, he gave her a warm smile that reminded her of sunlight lancing through the darkness she carried inside herself.

Wes reached out and grasped Maggie's upper arm. She looked absolutely whipped. Her hair spilled across her shoulders in brazen defiance of Navy regulations. She looked magnificent in his eyes, regardless.

Maggie tried not to misinterpret Wes's hand on her arm. Her heart did, though. "When did you finish your report?" Maggie asked, walking with him toward the doors.

"About a half hour ago." Wes glanced down at her. "You must either have been slow or have written a book in there," he teased.

She quirked her mouth. "It was hard to think, to put things together in an order that, hopefully, the board will comprehend."

Wes walked Maggie out to the parking lot. There were few cars in it at this time of night. It was midnight. The Shore Patrol sentries halted at the door, and Wes thanked them. Darkness alternated with the sulfur lamplight in the lot as he spotted their parked vehicles.

Now that they were alone and out of earshot, Wes asked, "How are you feeling?"

"Like hell itself."

"You look beautiful in my eyes, Red."

Lifting her chin, Maggie drowned in his shadowed gaze, which smoldered with undisguised need of her. If only he meant it in the way she needed it to be. If only... "For once, I'm not going to take that as a line from you. I'm too tired to rise to the bait."

"Good. Because it was the truth, not a line. Listen, I'm going to drive you home. Don't fight me on this, Maggie. I'll pick you up tomorrow morning at 0900. That's when we've got to show up in uniform for the board of inquiry."

Maggie wanted to sink into his arms and just be held, but true to form, he didn't offer that. "Okay... Thanks, Wes."

Saying nothing, Wes tried to table his growing concern for Maggie's mental and emotional condition. He already knew that sick bay and the psychiatrist had given them both a clean bill of health to fly again. Maggie would have to wait a week before going up— a mandatory period of time invoked for anyone who'd experienced a crash. Other than that, they felt she was fine. Wes disagreed.

Maggie climbed stiffly into his car. After belting up, she lay back and closed her eyes. Shortly thereafter, she fell asleep, oblivious to everything.

Wes glanced at Maggie from time to time as he drove. Lights twinkled from homes they passed along the highway. Above him, the low, stratus clouds that could sometimes plague the San Diego area were in evidence. His gaze came back to rest on Maggie. Despite her clean profile, he could see the emotional toll of the crash reflected in her features. There were still dark circles under her eyes. Her mouth, which should have relaxed when she slept, was still pursed in an uneven line that showed how much pain and worry she continued to hold inside.

Reaching over, Wes gently picked up one of her hands and placed it on his thigh. No longer did he lie to himself about her. He knew it was love. But, what the hell was he going to do about it? If the board cleared them of fault, Maggie would be thrown right back into the same demanding flight schedule of preparation for Red Flag. He wondered if she was emotionally ready to tackle that kind of pressure. His gut screamed no. His fingers tightened around her limp hand.

At her apartment, he woke Maggie. She appeared disoriented in the car, so he walked her up the steps and opened the door for her.

"I'll pick you up at 0820," Wes told her, keeping a hand on her because she wasn't walking a very straight line.

"Yeah . . . fine. . . ."

"Will you be okay, Red?"

Maggie responded despite her utter exhaustion. She reached out, placing her hand on his broad chest. "I'm just beat, Wes. That's all." Beat and hurting because I love you, and you won't ever love me. She removed her hand—the last thing she wanted to do. If only she could rest her head against that powerful chest where that caring heart lay . . . "Thanks. I'll see you tomorrow morning."

Wes closed the door after Maggie entered her apartment. What he wanted to do was stay the night with her and hold her. He knew it was what she needed right now. Making love to Maggie could come later. Right now, she reminded him of Annie when she hurt herself; at those traumatic times, Annie needed comforting arms around her to make everything better.

Turning, Wes ambled back to his parked car. In less than twelve hours, they would know their fate. As he climbed in and drove off toward his apartment a couple of miles down the road, he reflected that his career wouldn't be affected much, one way or another. No. Maggie's career was the one on the line. What had she put in her report? Was it the same as his? The board would leap at any little discrepancy that existed between the two reports and try to make something out of it.

His scowl deepened. How was Maggie going to hold up under their brutal inquisition? Would she? Why had the psychiatrist pronounced her fit to fly again, when something deep inside told him she wasn't ready at all? What was he sensing about her? Fear of flying again? Often, pilots had to overcome their fear and climb back in the cockpit anyway. Tomorrow morning was going to be brutal on Maggie, and dammit, Wes wanted to protect her in some way. But it was going to be impossible.

Maggie and Wes sat at a small table in front of three senior officers who composed the board of inquiry. With them was a provost marshall and an attorney. A yeoman sat off to one side, acting as court reporter.

Although Maggie was in her light blue summer uniform of skirt and blouse with low black heels, she wished for her familiar one-piece flight suit. It was more comfortable. She was perspiring heavily and had the irritating urge to wipe her upper lip dry. Her boss, Commander Parkinson, was one of the members on the board—in her mind, her only friend. The other two officers, both fellow pilots stationed at Miramar, were grim-faced.

Wes sat, outwardly relaxed, his hands clasped on the table as he waited for Commander Hodges to speak. But he felt the terrible tension in Maggie. His heart was breaking for her—she shouldn't have to go through this torture right now. And trying to guess the board's reaction to the crash was an impossibility.

Hodges cleared his throat. "Lieutenant Donovan, I want you to go over what happened for us one more time. Give us a verbal picture... a blow-by-blow of what happened."

Wes's eyes widened. What the hell were they doing that for? He glanced over at Maggie. Did she know this was an unusual request? Apparently not.

"Sir," Wes spoke up, knowing he shouldn't, but doing it anyway. "Isn't it unusual to ask the pilot to repeat *everything* that happened all over again? Isn't that what our reports are for?"

Hodges stared over at him. "Lieutenant Bishop, there's a discrepancy in your reports about what happened up there. It's up to the board to find out more about it."

Maggie's eyes rounded. Her heart started beating a staccato in her breast. A discrepancy! Immediately Maggie wondered what they'd found. Licking her lips, her mouth dry with tension, she began talking in a low voice. She tried to recall every detail of the flight for the board. Wes was tense, and once, during her dissertation, he gave her a look filled with such care, that it gave Maggie the shot of courage she needed to go on.

Midway through her discourse, Wes groaned to himself. Maggie had mistakenly noted the golden eagle as being on his radar. In his report, he'd referred to it as a ghost, nothing more. Sweat broke out on his brow. He knew what the board was thinking. They thought he'd probably lied and covered up this bit of information to protect Maggie. Damn! Nothing could be further from the truth, but would they believe him and not her? If they didn't, Maggie's career could be over right now.

It was agony to sit there for the half hour while Maggie faithfully repeated the accident sequence. Wes saw Hodges make several notes. He wasn't their friend. In fact, Wes recalled that Hodges was vehemently opposed to women flying combat at all. And Hodges was the one convening this board. His decision could ax Maggie. The only hope was to persuade the other two commanders to side with him on this, and outvote Hodges.

"Thank you, Lieutenant Donovan." The room was eerily quiet. He honed in on Maggie.

"Lieutenant, you've repeated your report faithfully to the letter. Normally, we'll get two slightly varied accounts from the pilot and RIO. The one on paper, and then what they recall twenty-four hours later. But you've recalled every detail."

"Thank you, sir." Maggie moved uncomfortably, feeling Wes's building tension. What was going on? Why was he looking at her like that? Had she said something wrong?

Hodges held up both reports to them. "Now, Lieutenant Donovan, according to Lieutenant Bishop, your RIO, he saw only a ghost on his radar. In your report, you said he identified and reported an eagle on his radar screen. Now, this may be a very minor detail, but it's a very large one in determining if the crash was your fault or not.''

Maggie drew in a breath. She jerked a look over at Wes. His eyes flashed with anger as he leaned forward, his elbows on the table.

''Commander Hodges, I'm afraid Lieutenant Donovan has overstepped her territory here. I reported a ghost on my radar, nothing more. At no time did I confirm it was an eagle.''

Maggie realized her error, and a terrible, sinking sensation flooded her. She didn't like the gleam in Hodges's gray eyes. ''He's correct, Commander Hodges. I was wrong. I shouldn't have put it in my report that way. We knew it was a golden eagle seconds before it smashed into the cockpit canopy. Wes did report a ghost on the scope, that's all.'' Would they believe her?

Hodges laid down the reports in front of him. ''Changing your story now, Lieutenant Donovan?''

Fist clenched, Wes said, ''Sir, don't you think that Lieutenant Donovan is still recovering from this crash? I don't see how either of us is going to recall every last detail or in what order some of them happened. I saw a ghost on my scope, nothing more.''

''Unfortunately, the flight recorder in the fighter would confirm or deny your observation, Lieutenant Bishop. Once we locate the plane and recover the recorder, we can prove your statement one way or another.''

Frustration thrummed through Wes. Dammit, Hodges was going to try and hang Maggie for her report error. Then, he made a decision that would probably affect the rest of his life. The love he held for Maggie could easily be destroyed by what he was about to do. His heart tore, and Wes had never felt as miserable as he did in that moment of decision.

"You're overlooking one thing," Wes told the board in a low voice. "Lieutenant Donovan has a past history of bossing her RIO around. If you question Lieutenant Brad Hall, he'll confirm that Lieutenant Donovan often overrode his observations and decisions. I saw a ghost on my screen. If Lieutenant Donovan wants to call it an eagle, that's her privilege. But, dammit, I'm the RIO! I'm the one with eight years of training to know what I'm looking at on those screens. She's not."

Maggie's mouth fell open, startled by the anger and vehemence in Wes's steely cool voice. She stared at him, unable to believe she was hearing him say these things about her.

"Now, if this board wants to believe the pilot in this case—who has *no* radar screens in front of her—then that's your problem. I know what I saw. It was a ghost. At no point after I saw it on-screen for that brief second, did I think it was something tangible. I know eagles don't fly above ten thousand, and in my mind, I'd already dismissed the idea of a bird at thirteen thousand feet. It was *my* determination, gentlemen, that we could remain at thirteen thousand. If Lieutenant Donovan wanted to change flight altitude, it was up to her. She chose to remain at thirteen

thousand based upon *my* assessment of the situation.
If there's any blame to be spread here, it's to me.
Frankly, no RIO would have been able to say for sure
what that ghost was. It's impossible, and I believe this
board knows that.''

Wes sat back, hurting badly for Maggie. God, he'd
just stabbed her in the back by feigning distrust in her.
He saw disbelief, injury and then anger in her eyes as
she stared over at him. He felt like hell, but it was the
only option he saw for saving her from Hodges, who
wanted to end her career.

''Well,'' Hodges drawled, ''is that true, Lieutenant
Donovan? Did Lieutenant Bishop report a ghost and
not an eagle?''

''Yes, sir, he did,'' Maggie whispered tautly. How
could he accuse her of such things? How! Anger
shattered through her. Why had he embarrassed her
like this in front of the board? It was a trick Hall
would employ, but never Wes. Confused, Maggie sat,
her hands tightly clasped in her lap, pain bursting
through her heart. His actions had proven all too
clearly to her that theirs was strictly a professional relationship. If he liked her, even a little, he wouldn't
have hanged her like this.

Hodges looked at his cohorts. ''Well, gentlemen?''

Commander Perkins, a man in his late forties,
leaned forward. ''Unfortunately, I've heard talk about
Lieutenant Donovan's need to run the show in the
cockpit before. This isn't the first report of her in-
ability to share duties and responsibilities in the cockpit.''

"Lieutenant Donovan has a problem in that area," Parkinson confirmed. "But, I feel she's working at trying to solve this need to control enough that we should clear her and Lieutenant Bishop and let them get on with training for Red Flag. Frankly, I don't think any RIO could unequivocally have seen that ghost on the radar and positively identified it as an eagle."

"Very well," Hodges said. "Lieutenants Donovan and Bishop, you're cleared of any charges. However, Lieutenant Donovan, what will go into your jacket will be an official reprimand that you tend to override the decision of your RIO, and that you should work to correct this deficiency. Understand?"

Maggie nodded. "Yes, sir." The words came out flat, emotionless. Inwardly she seethed, so angry at Wes that she could barely think straight. Wait until she got him alone!

"A week from now," Parkinson added, "you will both be returned to flight status. Your orders are to continue to work toward Red Flag, which is still two months away. Dismissed."

"Just what the hell did you think you were doing in there?" Maggie demanded, rounding on Wes once they were out in the parking lot and away from other eyes and ears.

Wes halted at his car and opened the door for her. "Maggie, calm down. I didn't do it to hurt you. Let's talk once we get out of here." Wes lifted his head and looked around. Under no circumstances did he want their heated argument to be heard.

Maggie sat boiling in the seat as Wes drove them off base and toward their apartments. "How could you? You gutted me in there! No way did I second-guess you on that ghost!"

Wes clung to his patience. "Listen to me, Maggie. I *had* to do it. Don't you see?"

"The only thing I see is that you stabbed me in the back! You're just like Hall!" Her voice cracked.

Wincing, Wes whispered, "Stop and think a minute, will you? I know you're emotionally upset over this crash. You're still in shock, as far as I'm concerned. That damned board shouldn't have convened so soon. They should've let you rest up, but they didn't. When you put down in your report that I saw an eagle on my screen, the board thought that I was covering for you, lying for you."

"What?" Maggie gave him a startled look.

"You had no right to put down on your report that I said the ghost was an eagle, Maggie. You overstepped your bounds on that one. I think you put it down, not realizing what you were writing. Hodges is antiwomen, in case you didn't see it. He was inferring that I was lying to protect your mistake in the cockpit. He wanted to hang you, Maggie. Didn't you see that?"

Rubbing her temple, she whispered, "No!"

"If I hadn't brought up the fact that Hall had trouble with you, and pretended a little bit of rightful outrage in there, Hodges was going to deep-six you, Maggie. Your career would be over. Over! Is that what you want?"

She glanced over at his taut, set face, his stormy blue eyes. "No, of course not!"

"If I hadn't put on that wounded-male act in there, believe me, Hodges was going to fry your tail but good, and I knew it. So did Commander Parkinson. Did you see the way he dovetailed into my explanation and backed me up on it? If he hadn't, Hodges was going to remove you from Red Flag for sure. Dammit, you've worked too hard for too long to have everything ripped away from you just because you screwed up on your flight report!"

Maggie absorbed his emotional explanation. All she wanted to do was turn into Wes's arms. It was a sunny day, with white clouds dotting the light blue sky. The hills of Poway were dark green with orchards of avocados here and there. But Maggie hardly saw any of it, so badly was she hurting inside.

"I thought," Maggie whispered, "you were doing it to keep your career clean."

Wes held on to his frayed patience. "My career involves flying with a pilot, Maggie. In this case, you. I would never push the blame on you or any pilot to keep my record clean. Hasn't the past month of flying together proved anything to you, Maggie? You were beginning to trust me, to give me back the control an RIO needs to operate at peak efficiency in the cockpit with you. Yes, you did ride roughshod on Hall. But I suspect, knowing him as I do, that you had to or he'd have screwed up your pilot responsibilities. And that's something you knew couldn't happen."

Risking everything, Wes reached over to claim Maggie's hand. Her fingers were frighteningly cold.

"Honey, believe me, I would never knowingly embarrass you. I'm proud of who you are and what you do for a living. No one's prouder than me. But I couldn't let Hodges sink your career. I scrambled mentally to find something—anything—to save you. I think I'm the only one who realizes what this crash has done to you, how much it's shaken you up. If they'd given you recovery time, I don't think you'd have put the eagle in your report as being seen on my radar screen. I think you'd have reported a ghost, just as I did."

Tears squeezed into Maggie's eyes. Wes's actions all made sense up to a point. Why had he called her honey? Why was he holding her hand? "I understand what you did, Wes," she croaked.

His heart took a skyrocketing leap. Dividing his attention between driving and watching her anguished profile, he whispered, "You do? You honestly know why I did it?"

Sniffing, Maggie wiped away the tears. "I'm so screwed up inside, Wes. I don't even know which way is up, right now. If you hadn't waved that reason in front of Hodges, he'd have blamed me for the crash, thinking you lied to protect me."

An incredible avalanche of relief spread through Wes. He lifted her hand, kissing the back of it. "Thank God. I was praying you'd realize what I was doing. You looked so angry back there—like you could kill me."

Avoiding his searching gaze, Maggie admitted, "I was pretty upset." His hand felt good, and she didn't want to release it.

"Listen, we can use this week to good advantage, Maggie. I've been thinking about our training schedule. But I don't want to talk about it now. Just stay home for today and rest up. Some other time, I'll toss my ideas out to you."

A fear started deep inside Maggie, and she broke out in a heavy sweat. What was going on? Focused on her own anxiety reaction, she didn't hear what else Wes was saying. When he removed his hand, the fear choked her, and she gasped.

"Maggie?" Wes turned into her apartment complex. She was pale; all the blood had drained from her face. "What's wrong?"

"Nothing... nothing..."

Wes parked the car and looked at her searchingly. "Are you sure?"

Maggie gave a jerky nod of her head, as the fear overwhelmed her to the point where she could taste it in her mouth. Fumbling for her purse, she got out of the car. "I'll see you at Ops tomorrow," she said, her voice low and off-key.

Frowning, Wes watched Maggie hurry up to her first-floor apartment. What the hell had happened? One minute she was fine, the next, she'd looked as if she were going to faint. Gripping the steering wheel, he waited until Maggie disappeared inside before leaving. Wes felt as if he were battling a many-headed hydra with Maggie, unable to define all that was going on inside that head and heart of hers.

The only thing, he mused as he drove on to his apartment, that remained tenuous between them was the kiss, the bared emotions they'd shared with each other after the crash. Maggie's response to his kiss had been *real*. Her hunger had matched his own. It had happened. Could he walk the fine line with Maggie to help her get back on track with her flying? She was so brittle right now that Wes was afraid the crash had in some way shattered her confidence. There was no way to tell until they got in the cockpit, and that was a week away.

Running his fingers through his hair in an aggravated motion, Wes thought he had never felt this helpless. Would a week on the ground help or hurt Maggie? Did she fear getting back in the air? And if she did, how would it affect the tentative, fragile relationship he wanted so desperately to pursue with her?

Chapter Nine

"How are you feeling?" Wes stood with Maggie at the bottom of the ladder of the F-14. It was to be their first flight after being off on waivers for a week. Maggie had been pointedly silent all morning, her normal joking and lightning wit nowhere to be seen. The sun was just brimming the horizon. The day was clear and the air smooth for good flying.

"Okay." Maggie pulled on the Nomex flight gloves. Her hands were shaking like leaves. It hurt to lie to Wes, but she couldn't stand on the ramp bawling like a baby because she was scared to enter the cockpit, to fly again.

Chantal came around the nose of the plane. "We're ready, Ms. Donovan."

"F-fine." Maggie slowly turned, gazing to the top of the cockpit that towered above her. It looked so far away, so tall. For the first time in her life she didn't see the sleek lines of the Tomcat as beautiful. Instead, all she saw was a massive fighter capable of killing her.

Wes motioned for Chantal to leave them, and the crew chief nodded, concern evident in her eyes. When they were alone, Wes stepped to Maggie's side and placed his hand on her shoulder.

"If it makes any difference, I'm scared, too, Maggie," he told her in a low voice.

Her eyes darted to his, and then she quickly looked away. Such a huge portion of her wanted to admit her fear to Wes, but she couldn't. Now she knew what Molly had meant by fear. The feeling had gutted her for the past seven days, getting worse with each hour, so that she hadn't slept well for the last three nights. Worse, Wes hadn't contacted her all week. If he really cared for her, he would have. For the first time in her life, Maggie knew what a broken heart felt like.

"I'm fine," Maggie forced out between her teeth, and she reached up, wrapping her fingers around the aluminum ladder and placing her flight boot on the first step. If she stayed there two seconds longer, Maggie knew she'd collapse against Wes. And he'd think less of her for it.

Wes watched Maggie move jerkily up the ladder and into the cockpit. Her mouth was tight, her eyes narrowed. There was such anguish mirrored in her green eyes that it sickened him. She was wrestling with some very real monsters right now. Slowly he moved up the ladder and into the back seat. Chantal and another crewman circumspectly reappeared and came to help them buckle up.

To Maggie's consternation and growing frustration, she couldn't seem to do anything right. She had to go over her ground checklist twice. She eyed the throttles, afraid to touch them. Forcing herself, she gave the signal for engine start-up. But instead of the powerful growl that shook the aircraft making her feel safe, Maggie felt the opposite. Sweating, she wiped her upper lip and brow repeatedly with the back of her gloved hand.

"Preflight list complete," Wes said over the intercom.

"Roger." Maggie pushed the button that would bring down the Plexiglas canopy. Suddenly bits and pieces shuttered in front of her open eyes: the eagle smashing into them...blood and bone everywhere around her...the cockpit awash, with crimson liquid coating her instrument panel...

"...Maggie?"

"...What? Yes?" Maggie tried to shake the crash sequence out of her mind. Wes had been speaking to her, and she hadn't heard a word he'd said.

"Why don't you just taxi this bird out to the end of the runway and get the feel of her? This can be a short flight. We don't have to fulfill the training schedule. One day isn't going to hurt us."

The suggestion sounded heavenly, but Maggie was afraid not to train. "Wes, we've been grounded a week. Missing another day *will* impact on us."

Sighing, Wes sat back and said nothing. The wobble in Maggie's voice was real. Would she freeze at some point? Cause a crash? What the hell was going on in her head?

As they taxied out to the end of the airstrip in the crisp morning air, Wes thumbed his intercom button.

"You know, this reminds me of getting thrown off a horse. You gotta climb back on or the fear will stop you from ever trying to ride again."

Wes's soothing, deep voice took away some of her fear. Maggie concentrated as never before. One mistake on her part could kill them. "Don't talk to me right now," she rasped. "I've got to concentrate."

"Roger." Wes heard the carefully concealed panic in Maggie's voice. He ached to help her, but once again, this was something she had to face and tackle on her own.

At the end of the strip, Maggie got clearance for takeoff. Sweat dripped from her, and her breathing was growing ragged. Gasping for air through the oxygen mask on her face, she thought she sounded like a fish out of water. A part of her brain ordered her to take off, but she remained frozen.

Wes scowled, realizing that something was wrong. "Maggie?"

No answer. The jet continued to sit, engines on idle, at the end of the runway.

"Maggie, talk to me. What's wrong?"

The sweat ran into Maggie's eyes. She blinked rapidly as the salt stung them.

Cursing, Wes thumbed the intercom button again. "Maggie, snap out of it!"

Wes's thundering order made her jerk outwardly. "I—I can't!"

Wincing, Wes ignored the cry in her voice. "Now listen to me, Donovan. You put your hand on those twin throttles and ease them forward to takeoff speed. Got that?"

Woodenly, Maggie did as he ordered in a voice low with fury. The engines' whine increased, the fighter shook and trembled around her like a living thing. She pressed her booted feet hard against the rudders to anchor the fighter, which seemed to want to leap down the runway and out of her control.

"Now, release rudders. Maggie, you hear me?"

Shame flowed through her, mingling with the fear that kept her almost immobile. "Y-yes."

"You're doing fine. Don't let the fear stop you. Let it stay with you, but react. Do you hear me? React."

"What if I can't fly?"

"That's ridiculous! You've got over a thousand hours in this jet! Release rudders, dammit! You're holding up all flights wanting to use this runway to land. Do it! *Now!*"

Wes was pressed back into his seat as the fighter surged forward in a thunderous roar. His mouth grew dry. Was Maggie in charge? Or was she in some kind of daze of fear, letting the fighter guide itself? Automatically he placed his hands on the arms of his ejection seat, his fingers near the triggers beneath each arm—just in case.

They were up! Maggie jerked the stick back upon rotation. The fighter bounced, nose up, almost into a stall position. Immediately she pushed the stick forward to bring the nose back down to an acceptable angle. The myriad of gauges confused her wide, searching eyes. Which to look at first? What altitude was she at?

For the next half-hour of flying toward the restricted airspace, Maggie wrestled between staying airborne and capitulating to the smothering, all-consuming fear that threatened to swallow her alive. The only things that kept her from going off the deep end were Wes's sharp commands, interspersed with his calming, supportive comments. She seesawed between his cold fury over the intercom and his warm praise each time she did something right. And every time, Maggie had to remind herself that what Wes was doing was professional, not personal. It hurt like hell to know that.

In the restricted zone, Maggie made a mess of things. She could do nothing right. Fortunately, she was only up against Dana, and every time she blew a test, Dana didn't reprimand her. Instead, she gave her support and urged Maggie to try again. By the end of the two hours, all Maggie wanted to do was go home and land. Washed out, she somehow managed to make a rookielike landing back at Miramar.

As the canopy rose, Wes quickly unbuckled his harnesses. Wes ordered Chantal and her crew to leave as soon as they'd placed the ladders next to each cockpit. Chantal gave him a worried look, but did as he asked. Climbing down his ladder and up the ladder leading to Maggie's cockpit, Wes saw the tortured look on her wan features.

"Let me help you," Wes murmured, unsnapping several buckles on the harness that kept her pinned tightly against the seat.

Maggie could only sit there, numb with exhaustion. Wes's nearness gave her hope, offered her some stability. "I—I flew like a rookie."

"You flew like a pilot who was scared after a crash," Wes corrected gently, placing the harnesses aside so she could get out of the cockpit. Maggie's flight suit was completely drenched in sweat, and he became alarmed. He'd seen some pilots sweat a lot— huge, dark splotches beneath their armpits and down the center of their chest—but never to this degree. Maggie hung her head; her lower lip trembled.

"It's all right, Red," he soothed, cupping her chin and forcing her to look up at him. "You did fine for a first flight. It was a bitch, but you did it. I'm proud of you." Sweet God, but he wanted to lean over and taste her lips once again, to kiss her. The urge was almost painful.

The fierce, burning light in his eyes made Maggie want to cry. "I—I've lost it, Wes. Whatever I had— that confidence—it's gone. Gone!"

"Naw, it's still there," he soothed, smoothing his thumb across her cheek. The need to love her was nearly overwhelming Wes. "It will come back, I promise you. This is temporary. I've seen it happen before."

His hand on her cheek was a painful reminder of what would never be. As he removed it, anguish threaded through Maggie. Slowly she collected her items for her duffel bag and stowed them with shaking hands. "I don't know, Wes. I screwed up on every dogfight and lost. God, I'm glad it was Dana out there. If it'd been a man, he'd come back here and spread it all over Miramar...."

Wes took her duffel bag. "No one's going to say anything about it, Maggie," he promised her grimly. "Come on. Do you feel like climbing out?"

With a short, nervous laugh Maggie looked down at her legs. "I feel like I've got spaghetti for legs."

"Take your time. I'll just stand here chatting with you until you feel strong enough to move."

Grateful beyond words, Maggie closed her eyes. Wes could have left her sitting alone in the fighter, and everyone in her crew would have known about her condition. She pulled off the Nomex gloves—her hands were damp from perspiration. The ninety-degree heat only made her sweat more; but it was a dry heat and for that, Maggie was thankful. Finally she tested her legs.

"I think I can make it now. Thanks, Wes."

Standing at the bottom of the ladder, his hand outstretched in case Maggie's knees buckled as she clumsily clambered down, Wes wasn't so sure.

"I've got you," he whispered as her feet touched the ramp. Maggie collapsed momentarily against him. Just the fleeting touch of her body against his evoked heated memories of their two nights in each other's arms. Pushing those feelings aside, Wes helped Maggie to stand on her own. There was no doubt she was ashamed of herself. And, sadly, in his opinion, there was no need for her to feel that way.

With a soft sound, she gave in to her need to be held by him, even if for a split second. His fingers moved coaxingly along her tired, tense shoulders, easing the stress from them. Eyes closed, Maggie selfishly absorbed his fleeting touch and embrace.

"The van's waiting to take us to Ops," he told her, not wanting to let her go, but knowing he must. If the flight crew or someone else saw them holding each other, it wouldn't be good for their careers—particularly Maggie's. Unhappily, Wes released her. When her lashes swept upward to reveal her glorious green eyes, he groaned.

Nodding jerkily, Maggie eased out of his grip. Surprisingly, Wes refused to take his hand off her arm as he walked her toward the vehicle.

Maggie went through the motions of postflight filling out a debrief form in the quiet of one of many rooms at Ops. Wes had gotten her a cup of coffee, but it hadn't helped her nerves. Molly had come down to see her to offer support, and Maggie had needed her friend's quiet presence. Midway through her finishing her report, Wes left, saying he'd be back in a little while.

"Commander Parkinson?" Wes came to attention in front of his boss's desk.

Howard smiled. "At ease, Wes. What can I do for you?"

"Sir, may I close the door and speak privately with you?"

"Of course." Parkinson leaned back in his chair. "Have a seat."

"I'd rather stand, Commander." Wes took a deep breath. "Sir, I'm here on Maggie's behalf. I'm going to step on a lot of people's toes, but I've got to tell you that she's fragile after that crash. I'm genuinely worried about her.''

Howard frowned. ''The psychiatrist's evaluation said she was fine for flight duty.''

''I know, sir. But—'' Wes rubbed his jaw ''—this is a special circumstance. I feel I know Maggie well enough from flying with her the past month to say this. She's never failed at anything in her life. Losing a plane in a crash is failure of the worst kind for a pilot. In my opinion, Maggie's having a tougher time than most people would, coming back from this crash. She doesn't know how to cope with failure, so she's behind the eight ball worse than most people would be.''

''I see. . . .''

''I have a plan, sir. One that I hope will help her get over this fear of flying and get her back on track for Red Flag.''

''Go ahead.'' Howard sat up, listening closely.

''I'd like your permission to scrap the next two months of training flights and redo them with Lieutenant Molly Sinclair's guidance. I think we need fewer flight hours, and some days off in between these demanding flights. There is such a thing as being too ready, and that can work against you as much as not training enough. I think Maggie needs days off—time, if you will, to play.''

''Play?''

''Yes, sir. She needs less pressure, not more.'' And Wes went into great detail on how much responsibility Maggie had been carrying alone for the past two years. At the end, Parkinson agreed with him.

"Fine. Revise the training schedule and have Lieutenant Sinclair bring it to me for final approval. If Maggie doesn't snap back within a month, Wes, then I'm going to have to pull her out of the running for Red Flag. She's got to bounce back, or else. You understand that."

"Yes, sir. I do." But would Maggie? If she couldn't pull herself up by the bootstraps for Red Flag, she'd view herself as a total failure, and that could destroy her forever.

"Good. So, what kind of 'play' did you have in mind?" Parkinson smiled.

Wes smiled back. "Dumb things, silly things. I want to reintroduce her to flying in a different sort of way, so hopefully she'll gain back her flight confidence."

"You want tomorrow off for this 'play'?"

"Yes, sir."

Parkinson shrugged. "Lieutenant, if this works, I'll be putting a special recommendation in your personnel jacket."

Wes smiled tentatively, reading between the lines. If his plan didn't work, his jacket would also reflect his failed efforts. Coming to attention, he said confidently, "I'm sure it will work, Commander. Thanks for backing me on this."

As he walked down the hall, Wes whistled softly, feeling some of the pressure that he was carrying dissipate. He hated yelling at and cajoling Maggie when she was in the cockpit. He was using her anger against her to overcome her own fear, and that wasn't positive. In the long run, it would only serve to hurt her.

Crossing his fingers, he prayed that his plan would work. It had to, because he loved her.

Maggie was sitting in her dark blue silk bathrobe the next morning, drinking her first cup of coffee at 0600 when the doorbell rang. Who could it be? Frowning, she padded through the rooms and opened the front door. Wes stood there, dressed in a pair of casual ivory linen slacks and a lightweight crewneck sweater in subtle shades of blue, lavender and rose. The warm brown of his loafers gave him an aura of being expensively clothed, yet with understated taste and elegance.

Her pulse jagged. "Wes... What are you doing here? And why aren't you in uniform? Where's your flight suit?"

He grinned and placed his hands on his hips. "Did anyone ever tell you how gorgeous you look after just waking up?" It took every bit of his control not to reach out, tunnel his hands through her luxurious, recently brushed hair, then pull her into his arms and kiss her breathless.

Maggie gawked up at him, as his words slid like a velvet rasp across her sensitized body. She stepped aside, allowing him to come in, then shut the door. He continued to stand with that grin on his face and his eyes filled with mischief. "Okay, what's going down?" she asked suspiciously.

"You," he said, taking her by the arm and leading her down the hallway. "Better hurry and get dressed. Our plane's being fueled and our flight plan says we're leaving in an hour." He glanced at his watch. "Do you dress in a hurry?"

Openmouthed, Maggie stopped in the hall, wildly aware of his closeness and his hand on her arm. "Wes Bishop, what are you blithering about?" Her silken robe outlined her soft curves, and she took a step away from his overpowering, beckoning presence.

At last, a spark of the old Maggie he knew and loved was back. Wes smiled and reluctantly released her. He entertained the thought of taking Maggie to her bedroom and making slow, delicious love to her. The outline of her breasts against the blue robe was intoxicating. He wanted nothing more than to feel her softness beneath his exploring hands. "Today's a change of pace," he heard his voice echo as he fought to get control over his hard, throbbing body. "The uniform of the day is comfortable clothes suitable for a very fine restaurant I know up on Monterey Bay."

Her eyes widened. "Monterey Bay? That's four hundred miles north of here! And civilian clothes? Wes, slow down. You aren't making sense." Suddenly Maggie was on the defensive. Wes's bulk filled the hallway, making him appear larger than life. In her eyes and heart, he was the epitome of masculinity.

"Sure I am. And before you get that wonderful Irish temper of yours up and running, Commander Parkinson has approved today's flight. Now, I'm not going to tell you any more than that, except that it's officially okay to do it. I want this to be a surprise for you, Maggie. Something pleasant and fun to do. Go on, find a nice pair of slacks and a blouse to wear.

Maybe a light blazer because it gets chilly along the coast."

In mild shock, Maggie turned and went down to her room. She shut the bedroom door. What was Wes up to? What flight to Monterey Bay? An F-14 couldn't land there. The runways were far too short for such a jet. Disgruntled, she forgot about her building fear of going into Miramar to fly and hunted for slacks and a blouse as Wes had ordered.

When Maggie stepped into the living room, Wes gave a low, appreciative whistle and her cheeks turned a bright red beneath his appraisal. She wore an over-size cotton safari shirt and a split skirt in the same fabric. The rust-colored belt around her waist emphasized her slenderness. As he shifted his gaze down, he noticed she wore a pair of low-heeled shoes the color of the belt. The multicolored wooden beads of red, orange, green and yellow around her throat set off her loose, shining hair. She was scowling at him, however.

"Now, what's that look for, Red? You look like you don't trust me." Wes stepped forward and reached out, gripping her hand. "Come on, we're going to play today and have fun doing it," he promised her.

"I don't believe this," Maggie muttered. She sat in the pilot's seat of a single-engine Cessna-172 aircraft at Lindbergh Field, which paralleled San Diego Bay.

"Remember," Wes told her congenially, shutting his door and strapping in, "Commander Parkinson has okayed this flight."

Maggie closed her door. The instrument panel on the small civilian aircraft was simple and sparse compared to the array of instruments on her F-14. "Okay, what gives?"

"Fly us to Monterey Bay, Red." Wes patted the navigational maps spread across his lap. "I'll navigate and you fly, just like we always do."

"This is crazy!" She sat there, refusing to touch the yoke and throttle. Longing to ask him whether this plan was professional or personal, Maggie was torn as never before. To her, it was like a date—a crazy, wonderful date. But her head sourly reminded her that Wes's twice-yearly report had to reflect good grades if he was to get lieutenant commander, which he was up for this year. Of course, he had to get her back in the saddle of being comfortable flying; his rank could hinge on it.

"No, it's not."

Maggie held his warm blue gaze. "Why isn't it? Why is the commander reducing me to flying this thing? This is like flying a toy compared to the Tomcat, Wes!"

"Precisely my point. Do you feel that same fear you felt yesterday when you sat in the cockpit?"

Maggie checked herself out internally. "No," she muttered.

"This is therapy," Wes explained. "And my idea. I'm just glad Parkinson decided to go along with it." He gestured to the instruments in front of her. "You need your flight confidence built back up, Maggie. I wasn't going to see you sitting like a basket case in that F-14 cockpit two days in a row. Yes, this little airplane is like a toy compared to the monster you're used to hauling around in the sky, but you're also scared of failing again." A slight smile leaked through. "You can't fail in this, honey."

She stared hard at the instrument panel and the yoke in front of her, shattered. So, the plan he'd concocted was for career reasons only. His idea made sense to her, and then, shame came on its heels. "I could freeze up today, too," she whispered stubbornly.

Laughing, Wes reached over and touched her fiery red cheek. "No way."

His rumbling laugh was like sunlight embracing her when she felt so cold and alone. "If I did, we could crash. I could kill both of us."

"Oh?" he prodded innocently. More than anything, Wes realized Maggie needed to talk out her fears with someone. Just talking about them often helped relieve the terrible burden.

Maggie touched the yoke as if it were going to bite her. "I could crash. I could kill you. Not that I'd want to live. God, I couldn't stand two crashes in a row."

"The first crash wasn't your fault, Maggie."

"No, I guess it wasn't. But I still feel horrible about it. I keep feeling the eyes of every pilot on base accusing me silently of losing my plane. I did something that never should be done. They'll never forget it...or forgive me. I mean, look at the newspapers..." She closed her eyes and sat back, a tremulous sigh breaking from her taut lips. "I saw the national news last week the day after we got back to Miramar. Did you?"

"Yes," Wes admitted softly. There'd been a five-minute news presentation on their crash and the fact that Maggie was the first woman military pilot to lose her plane, even though she'd been cleared of any fault. The news story had made Wes furious. He'd hoped Maggie hadn't seen it, but now, seeing the anguish in her face and hearing the unadulterated pain in her voice, his anger soared. There was no way to protect her. All week—ever since they'd passed the board of inquiry—Wes had wanted to call or drop over to see Maggie. He'd fought himself almost hourly on that decision. Selfishly, he'd wanted—needed her. Professionally, it was proper not to be in her life that week, to allow her to rest up. Never had a week crawled by so miserably for Wes.

"That's past history now, Red," he whispered, gripping her cool hand. At least it wasn't damp with sweat—yet. "What else are you feeling?"

Just the tenor of Wes's voice broke the last of Maggie's reserve. She needed his touch right now, and she was amazed at his perception. For the next half hour, all her fears, her failures, spilled out of her in a torrent of words and feelings. Finally she grew silent and watched the gulls wheeling lazily above the dark blue waters of the bay.

"I wonder if sea gulls are ever afraid to fly," Maggie mused.

Wes stirred and forced himself to release her hand. Otherwise he was going to lean over, take her in his arms and kiss her so damn hard that she would melt into him and they'd become one living, breathing human being. The urge to do it was palpable, teasing. "I'll bet they do. Just like us. How do you feel now?"

Maggie realized that, miraculously, much of her fear was gone. "Better." She turned and held his gaze. "I don't know if I can fly, Wes. What if this fear strikes me again?"

"I'm sure it will. But every time it does, it'll get less intense, Maggie."

Feeling helpless, she touched the yoke with her long fingers. "I couldn't stand us to crash. You've got so much faith in me, Wes. I couldn't fail you a second time."

"Honey, failing isn't a sin—only a lesson to show us where we're weak. That's all." Maggie was painfully vulnerable and his love for her soared. She had trusted him with herself for the first time, and the feeling was simultaneously dizzying and humbling. "Fly us north and take your time. We've got all day. If you want to shoot some touch-and-go's up at Monterey Bay airport, do it. If you don't feel like it, don't. The whole aim of this is to make flying fun for you, the way it was before the crash. With time, your confidence will come back, Maggie."

She chewed on her lower lip, wanting to believe Wes's fervently spoken words. "I—I'll try."

"That's my Irish warrior talking now. Come on, I'll talk you through the preflight check. There's nothing to flying this little toy of ours."

Smiling tentatively, Maggie allowed her hand to remain on the yoke. "You sound like you know all about this aircraft."

"I do," Wes said, grinning. "I've got over a thousand hours in toys like this. When I got washed out of the Pensacola flight program after six weeks, I didn't give up. So what, if I didn't have what it took to be a jet jock? I still loved flying." He patted the yoke on his side of the plane. "Over the years I flew with airplane clubs on the naval air stations. I've got my single- and multiengine rating, plus a whole slew of other ratings, so that when I leave the Navy in six months, I'll start my career as an airline pilot. I've already got a job lined up with United Parcel Service. They're wanting to check me out to fly their jumbo jets overseas. I gave them a thumbs-up on that. So you see, my red-haired witch, you aren't going to crash. Even if fear grabs you by the throat and won't let you go, I'll be here to take over for you. Fair enough?"

Maggie was speechless for nearly a minute, staring at him in the gathering silence of the cabin. She was wrong about him worrying about getting his next rank, because he was leaving the Navy. Then what was his motivation behind this idea? If not professional, what? She closed her eyes and tried to sort out real reasons instead of her heart's blind ones. Maybe Wes *did* care a little bit for her. Or, her steel-trap mind reminded her coldly, Wes had to continue to fly with her. He didn't want to die in a crash, so it was in his best interests to get her flight confidence back.

Wes allowed her to watch him without taking offense, his smiled filled with guile, his eyes dancing with undeniable warmth. There was such confusion and question in her gaze. What was going on inside that pretty head of hers?

Finally, Maggie cleared her throat. "Why didn't you tell me this before?"

"What?"

"That you're a pilot."

He shrugged. "Didn't seem important."

"You've got as many hours as I have in the F-14."

"I suppose," Wes hedged.

"In my book, you're a fellow pilot, not just an RIO."

"I didn't tell you, Maggie, because I didn't want you to get defensive. When we started flying together, how would you have felt, knowing? Hall had already tried to tell you your job. With me in the back seat with equal flight hours, albeit different aircraft, you could have become very defensive."

"You're right," she admitted. "I probably would have, under the circumstances. Hall really made me touchy about my territory." Maggie gave him a grateful look. "You're a piece of work, Bishop. You know that?"

He grinned proudly. "Yeah?"

Maggie rolled her eyes. "And you know it. Okay, show me how to preflight this toy. Knowing you can take over if I freeze makes me want to try flying it now. Show me how to start it up."

Complying with her request, Wes saw a spark of life returning to Maggie's green eyes. He thanked the gods or goddesses of flight, the air, the clouds or whatever, that his decision to try this method had worked. Already, Maggie was beginning to behave more like her old self instead of a scared young child afraid of the dark.

It was a pleasure instructing Maggie because she picked everything up swiftly the first time around. As they took off from Lindbergh and flew north, Wes knew that in a very short amount of time, Maggie's flight confidence would return to its old levels. Not without an occasional stumble, because that's what failure did to one. Happily, he'd be there to coax her back onto her feet to try again. Yes, this day, this hour with Maggie was turning into a magic he'd never imagined. Now, Wes looked forward to their lunch at very magical Monterey Bay.

Chapter Ten

Over lunch at the Blue Gill in Monterey Bay, Wes enjoyed watching Maggie eat. She was getting back her usual ravenous appetite, thank God. The small, intimate seaside restaurant was packed at noontime, but they had the best table in the house: near the marble balustrade that overlooked the magnificent bay itself.

The sunlight danced prettily through the gnarled, twisted limbs of several Monterey pines that grew next to the highly polished pink marble railing. Wes found himself wanting to watch the colors of Maggie's hair change beneath the sunlight rather than eat. When she looked up, he grinned like a little boy.

"Caught in the act," he admitted.

Maggie tilted her head. "What do you mean?"

"Watching you."

She felt heat crawling up her cheeks. "That's not a very professional thing to do, Bishop."

"No. But it's fun, and you are worth looking at. Like fine wine, you should be savored."

Maggie put her fork down on the white china plate. She saw the mischievous glint in Wes's eyes. "Are you giving me one of your Irish-blarney lines now, or are you serious?" Her heart galloped in fear of his answer. She couldn't stand not finding out the truth from Wes. It was killing her.

"I'm serious. How do you feel about that?" He held his breath, afraid of her reply. Maybe his fierce need of her wasn't really a mutual thing. Maybe the kiss they'd shared up at Grayeagle was a fluke, a one-of-a-kind experience.

"Oh..." Maggie stared down at the portion of lobster still on her plate.

"That bad, huh?"

Her head snapped up. "No! I mean, that's nice."

"What is?"

She gave him a probing look. "That there's not only a professional relationship between us, but a little bit of a personal one, too."

Wes thought there was a hell of a lot more than a "little" personal feeling between them, but he didn't say it. Maggie was acting as jumpy as a doe that had been shot at. Why? "I think it's tough not to mix personal and professional in our business, don't you?"

"Well...yes."

"Are you comfortable with me sometimes looking at you with not such a professional eye?" he teased, touched by her blushing.

"I can live with it."

"That's nice."

Maggie managed a sour smile. "I really know how to shoot myself in the foot, don't I?"

Wes leaned over and captured her hand in his. "I just think the lady has had her mind on her career far too long and is a little rusty at personal repartee between a man and woman, that's all."

She tentatively squeezed his hand, feeling the immediate response of his fingers. With a sigh, Maggie allowed herself to hope—just a little bit—that Wes liked her. "I think you're right," she whispered.

"I've got an idea," Wes ventured.

"What?"

"Feel like flying some more? You did really well coming up here."

"Sure. What do you have in mind?"

He grinned and held her lovely green eyes that were soft with desire. "How about dinner and dancing in San Francisco tonight? We can get a couple of rooms at the Mark Hopkins Hotel and fly back tomorrow morning. I'm sure Commander Parkinson won't mind if you put in a few more flight hours."

Shocked, Maggie sat back and reclaimed her hand. "Dinner? Dancing?"

"You do like to dance, don't you?"

"Well...sure...but..."

"But what?"

Maggie was beginning to understand even more what Molly meant about living with fear. Now she was afraid to say anything more to Wes about his idea. What did he want from her? Or did he? Was this just part of his idea of playtime, or a chance to be alone with her in an intimate sort of way? She hated herself for her cowardice in not asking.

"It sounds wonderful," she said, meaning it.

"Great. Let me go make a phone call to Parkinson and clear it with him." Wes stood, smiling. "I'll be right back."

Maggie was discovering Wes was so wonderfully spontaneous. She never knew what he'd do or suggest next. And her heart still had hope in it—more than ever before, since their fateful meeting over a month ago. Suddenly Maggie was looking forward to San Francisco—and to being with Wes.

"It's hard to believe," Maggie whispered, dancing in Wes's arms. "We had lunch in Monterey Bay."

"And then you liked flying so much, you wanted to do more, so we ended up here in San Francisco for dinner tonight," Wes congratulated her, turning her on the dance floor that reflected a spectrum of lights from above. The music was from the fifties—ballroom dancing, the kind he liked. And he was delighted to discover that Maggie liked the same music.

Maggie smiled up into his shadowy features, a rare kind of love bubbling up through her as she danced lightly in his arms. "Our unexpected flight is going to raise some eyebrows back at Miramar, Bishop, and you know it."

"Commander Parkinson approved my plan. He doesn't care what you fly, as long as you fly. He also agrees that training should be three times a week, not seven."

Maggie laughed. She'd never felt so happy. "You're crazy, Wes. Completely and certifiably crazy!"

And you love me for it. But Wes didn't say those words. The flight up the coast of California after lunch had worked a miracle on Maggie. Landing at San Francisco International Airport, they took a taxi into the heart of the city, got two rooms at the Mark Hopkins Hotel, then bought clothes for a ritzy night out on the town.

"This is the kind of 'play' I was asking you about last month," Wes confided close to her ear as he skimmed his hand down her lower back as the slow music filtered around the many couples on the dance floor.

She smiled, moving with him, hotly aware of his hips against her own. Dressed in a dark blue suit, white silk shirt and red tie, Wes looked more like an executive corporate raider than an officer in the Navy. When his mouth moved against her temple, bussing her gently, Maggie turned her face toward his, wanting more—wanting him.

The brush of his male mouth against her lips sent a tremble through Maggie, and she responded to his tentative kiss, wanting to tell him in another language how much she loved him. As Maggie drowned in the splendor of his mouth fitting firmly against hers, she recalled Molly's words about love; about taking risks and reaching out, no matter how scared she was.

Hadn't Wes taught her today about overcoming fear and successfully dealing with failure?

"Mmm... You taste like fresh strawberries and cream, Red," he whispered against her mouth, feeling her smile. Wes gloried in the emerald gold of Maggie's eyes as her lashes lifted to reveal her feelings. His grip on her tightened. He wanted to make love with her—nothing had ever felt more right.

"And you taste like peach melba," she teased, wanting to kiss him again—more deeply, longer.

Wes read her desire in her lustrous green eyes. "Maggie, I want to love you. Here. Tonight." His heart thudded hard in his chest. She might turn him down. There was every reason for her to do just that. They had to work together for another two months. Could they separate their personal feelings for each other from their demanding work? He saw surprise register in her eyes.

Was she dreaming this? His request was so sudden, so unexpected. Maggie searched his now serious features. Was it the atmosphere, the fact that they were alone, which had prompted Wes to ask her? She'd accepted that he liked her. How much? was really the crux of the question. Her liking for him had turned to love overnight. Would their lovemaking be a one-night stand, a fleeting touch of mind, heart and body? He'd be gone in two months—to disappear forever from her life. Maggie had never played those kinds of games. They weren't her style and not what she wanted out of life.

As she gazed deeply into Wes's darkened eyes, her heart and body screamed at her to take the risk. "Wes, I'm afraid...."

"Yeah, so am I." And then his mouth quirked at an angle. "But I want you more than my fear of not having you."

"What about our jobs?"

"You mean, can we separate our personal feelings from the flying we have to do?"

"Yes."

He shrugged. Maggie felt so good in his arms. She wore a romantic floral chintz dress with a Pilgrim collar set off with a pink bow, and puffed sleeves. Tonight, she looked like a lovely teenage girl with those freckles across her cheeks instead of that so-very-serious woman combat-pilot he knew. "I'm willing to try. How about you?" His throat constricted as his gaze fell to the long, slender neck that he wanted to worship with kisses. Would she be as velvety smooth as he imagined beneath his mouth and exploring hands? Wes ached to find out.

A tremor passed through Maggie as he leaned down, kissing the point where her neck intersected with her jaw. The tiny, light kiss sent messages speeding through her taut, aware body. "I—I don't know."

"Do you like me?"

"Yes."

"Ever entertained the thought of going to bed with me?"

She grinned at his rakish smile. "Too many times for my own good."

"Have you dreamed about me?"

"Yes. And you?"

"Yeah, but I can't tell you about them. They're all R-rated."

Laughing throatily as Wes whirled her around in a circle just as the music ebbed to a halt, she whispered, "Yes, I want to love you, too...."

As they made their way from the dance floor, through the lobby and to the bank of elevators, Maggie felt as if she were in some kind of trance. Dana had confided to her after marrying Griff that every time they made love, it was as if she were in a wonderful, unraveling dream. That was how Maggie felt now.

She followed Wes into his room wrapped in a euphoria she'd never experienced before. Nothing had prepared her for the way the world drew to a halt around her as Wes slowly undressed her. The room was dark except for light from the sparkling city outside the hotel. He had already slipped off his shoes and gotten rid of his tie. Standing inches away from him as she freed each button on his silk shirt, she could feel the heat of him and the tension that swirled around them.

"When I first met you," Wes murmured as he unbuttoned the back of her dress, "I thought you were the most intriguing-looking woman I'd ever met." He smiled down into her eyes, dizzied by the passion he saw smoldering in them. Easing the dress off her shoulders, Wes glimpsed the pale pink silk teddy beneath it and he groaned. "I felt like the luckiest guy in the world—getting to spend eight or ten hours a day with you. I almost felt guilty about it. Almost..." And he trailed a series of light, butterfly kisses along the length of her neck to her shoulder, then gently pulled the strap of the teddy aside.

Maggie sighed audibly as his mouth continued down, down, until her breath caught in her throat. The silk teddy dropped to the floor and she leaned toward him, wanting, needing his continued touch.

Wes groaned as Maggie melted into his arms. He picked her up and gently deposited her on the bed beside him. Her red hair flowed across the white quilted bedspread like animated flame. He wanted to tell her he loved her, knew he couldn't. Not yet. Probably never. No, tonight was for Maggie—a part of her ongoing healing process. Instinctively, Wes knew that loving her, giving her this intense emotional outlet, would help her even more.

As she moved her hand across his naked chest, he closed his eyes, content to allow her to explore him, all of him. There was no hurry. No, not tonight. Even in the shadows he could see the burning gold and emerald in Maggie's eyes, that familiar hunterlike intensity coupled with a new searing passion. Only this time, he was her target. A smile tugged at Wes's mouth as she leaned over him. He threaded her silky hair through his fingers as her mouth met and melted against his. The moisture of her ragged breath, the sweetness of her mouth and the molding of her firm curves against him all conspired to make him lose touch with reality.

In the back of Wes's mind—what little of it was still functioning—he knew this might be the only time he'd ever get to love Maggie. She'd made clear that her profession came first, and that love, especially marriage, was out of the question for a long time to come.

"Come here," he coaxed huskily as he eased her on top of him, their flesh meeting and scorching upon contact. Her slender legs were like hot silk grazing his hips and thighs. Just the teasing brush of her heated, moist core made Wes groan. There was such luster and beauty in her eyes as she met and held his gaze. Her lips parted as he guided her down upon him.

Maggie cried out as she met and embraced him. All of him. His body felt powerful and tense beneath hers, as if he were going to explode. Maggie wanted this moment, this hour, to last forever. Her own cry of triumph mingled with his as she moved her fingers outward, tangling them in the black, thick hair that covered his chest. The sledgehammer pound of his heart connected with the palm of her hand. He moved his hips and she moaned, pleasure flowing through her in white-hot ripples.

"Give yourself to me, Maggie," he rasped, gazing into her sultry, half-closed eyes. "I want you—all of you.... Fly with me, my beautiful red-haired witch...."

The tilting of his hips sent a shower of heat welling through her like the building of a summer thunderstorm. Each movement, each rocking motion, tore away the last vestiges of control. Her senses, wildly alive, drank in all of him. She leaned over, capturing his mouth, tasting him deeply and feeling his hungry, demanding response. As his fingers tangled through her hair, holding her captive, he brought her in rhythm with himself.

The instant his mouth captured the hardened nipple of her breast, Maggie cried out in pleasure. The tension in her lower body built, like a thunderstorm, swelling and demanding. The night blended with her, and she became immersed in Wes, hot and melting, as he coaxed her toward the surging tidal wave of ultimate pleasure. It was so easy to trust him, to give herself over to his roving hands, his hungry mouth and strong, giving body. Her breath caught as fire exploded to life inside her. Dizzily she stilled in his embrace, caught up in the storm of lightning he'd unleashed deep within her. Almost simultaneously, she felt Wes tense and heard his groan—like the growl of a wild animal—telling her that he, too, was sharing the most wonderful gift they could give to each other.

Maggie sighed, feeling a good kind of tiredness as she lay in Wes's arms. Their bodies were still damp in the aftermath of their fiery lovemaking. Time had drawn to a halt. Nuzzling beneath his chin, she wanted nothing more from life than what she had now: Wes. How much she loved him.

Idly Wes ran his fingers down Maggie's arm, now thrown across his belly. Her thick hair lay across his chest like a crimson coverlet. "You're quite a woman, Maggie Donovan," he whispered. "Quite a woman."

She kissed his neck and then his collarbone. "I think we're pretty good together." Light streamed in through the floor-to-ceiling sheers, reflecting off the expensive antique furniture in their room. "I like the smell of you, the taste..."

A smile touched his mouth as he threaded thick strands of her hair through his fingers, watching them slowly drop and swirl back around her head and shoulders. "I like your ability to love. You're like a fire out of control."

"Is that your way of saying I'm wild?"

Chuckling, Wes gathered Maggie into his arms. "Wild and sinfully all woman." He kissed her damp brow, grateful that Maggie's spirit was back again.

Maggie put her arms around his neck, content as never before. "I've never felt so good, Wes," she admitted, getting serious now.

He felt her mood change—again like fire, never the same twice in any given moment. To Wes, that was part of Maggie's mystique. "You needed this," he told her.

I needed you. But in response, Maggie said nothing, just nodded her head. Loving Wes, she knew, wasn't an automatic guarantee of anything.

Wes was hotly aware of Maggie's body against his. "Everyone needs someone now and again," he teased gently. He'd like to have *her* forever.

With a grimace, Maggie whispered, "You're right. Before this, I never needed anyone, Wes. I did it all on my own. I succeeded because of the energy I put into it." Her eyes darkened. "Since the crash, I've begun to understand what Molly meant by being better off with a partner in a positive relationship. I just didn't have time for it. I thought it would distract my focus too much from my career and responsibilities."

He lay silent a long time, assimilating her admission. "It still might, Maggie. We'll sleep together tonight, maybe make love one more time before we have to leave tomorrow morning, but what happens after that is up to both of us."

Softly she answered, "I know..." She paused. "Wes, you've always supported me—from the day you arrived. Through everything, you were there. You never gave up on me. You didn't walk away, and you could have."

"I wouldn't walk away from you ever, Maggie. You don't leave someone you like in the lurch. You try to help them."

She closed her eyes, giving him a long hug. "Well, you sure helped me."

"Still scared?"

Opening her eyes, she smiled and lifted her head just enough to meet his smoldering blue gaze. "Yes, but I *want* to be scared with you. Okay?"

His heart hammered hard in his chest. Wes gently cradled her cheek against his hand. "Okay, Red, we'll take this one day at a time. Together."

It was more than she'd dared hope for. "Okay. Together. Molly's right: I don't know how to weave a personal relationship into the fabric of my career. I'm sure I'll make mistakes with you."

"So, we'll do it together the best we can. How's that sound?" Maggie looked exquisitely vulnerable in his arms, her eyes reflecting both her uncertainty and her courage to try—despite the fact that this, too, could fail. He loved her passionately for once again overcoming her fear.

Maggie pressed her lips on Wes's mouth, wanting to love him fiercely all over again, to tell him through her body's silent language that she loved him. "That sounds fine," she whispered against him.

Maggie awoke with the sun streaming in their east-facing window, its golden light making the room come alive in a blaze of beige, topaz and champagne colors. Wes stirred, tightening his arms around her as she stretched languidly beside him.

"Is it morning?" he asked thickly.

Giggling, Maggie replied, "Why don't you open your eyes and find out, Bishop?"

"Naw, I want this dream to continue. Magic only happens at night, didn't you know that? Daylight destroys it. So, I'll keep my eyes closed, and it'll still be night, and you'll stay in my arms."

Maggie smiled, thoroughly content. "Yesterday morning you said you were going to leave the Navy at the end of your enlistment."

Wes forced his eyes open. Maggie had propped herself up on one elbow and was studying him. Her hand moved lazily across his chest, tangling in the soft hair across it. He caressed her arm. "Yeah, that's right."

"For some reason I thought you were a thirty-year person, like me."

Blinking the sleep out of his eyes, Wes read between the lines of her statement. Wes knew how serious he was about Maggie. He loved her. He dreamed of a lifetime with her. But did she dream that, too? Wes studied her thoughtful features, thinking how beautifully her mussed hair framed her face and shoulders.

"When I didn't make it through flight school at Pensacola, I changed my career plans. I chose to make the best use of my time during the six years I had to stay in the Navy. I've used the time to get my pilot's license and other ratings to make it outside in the civilian world afterward. Being an RIO is something I do now. I like it, but I like flying better."

"You're really something else, Wes."

He smiled softly up at her serene features. All the tension and strain were erased from around her eyes and mouth. "Why?"

"There's so much to you!"

He snorted. "There is to every man. Why should it come as such a surprise to you, Maggie?"

"You're not like other men, Bishop, and you know it. Or, at least I do."

His grin was lazy and confident as he reached out, sliding his hands across her velvety, creamy-white shoulders. "And you're unlike any other woman I've known, Maggie Donovan. Now, come here. I want to love you one more time before we have to leave...."

"I think you've really come together on your flying," Dana congratulated Maggie as she walked with her and Wes toward the van near the Miramar hangar. "It's as if the crash made you better, Maggie."

"I wouldn't say that." Maggie traded a look with Wes, who walked easily at her side. In two months, they had indeed "come together," to use Dana's innocent expression. Her two closest friends knew of her relationship with Wes, but the secret was safe with them. No one at Miramar even suspected anything other than a professional tie between her and Wes.

Wes took their duffel bags and stowed them in the rear seat while the women boarded the van. "Well," he said, as he climbed in after them, "tomorrow we head to Nellis on Red Flag. Then we'll see how well we've put this together."

Maggie smiled. The early-October heat beat down on them, and the air-conditioning in the van was doing little to cool them off. Flight suits were notorious for holding heat because of their fire-retardant material.

"You excited, Maggie?" Dana asked, leaning forward, her arms resting across the back of her seat.

"Scared to death," Maggie answered honestly.

"Me, too," Wes added.

"So am I," Dana admitted.

"How about if we all be scared-to-death together?" Wes suggested.

Maggie settled back, enjoying Wes's closeness on the van's vinyl seat. The past two months had been a combination of heaven and hell. Heaven in Wes's arms each night at his or her apartment; and hell during the day trying to get back her flight confidence. Even now, Maggie couldn't fool herself. She still got the shakes when first entering the cockpit. And blips of the crash could strike at odd moments, even during critical dogfight sequences, throwing off her concentration. She wasn't flying as consistently as before the crash, and that could hurt their chances at Red Flag.

Dana tapped Maggie on the shoulder. "Hey, you know Molly's already a week late delivering Rachel.

But I talked to the midwife and doctor yesterday, and they didn't seem concerned." She smiled, excitement charging her voice. "Maggie, wouldn't it be something if Molly waits to have the baby until Cam gets home? He and Griff are due in San Diego the day after we get back from Red Flag."

"That would be the best thing that could ever happen," Maggie agreed with feeling. "I'd really like to be there for the birth the way we'd planned in the first place. I mean, we've trained with Molly, the doctor and midwife." Maggie applauded Molly's decision to have her baby at home and with a woman doctor and midwife present. Molly had the very firm opinion that birthing was a woman's realm, not a man's. However, she knew Molly was praying that Rachel would wait one more week, so Cam could be present to witness the birth of his daughter.

Maggie looked up. She saw the hangars with the hottest jets in the world parked outside them, and the crews working around their charges. Funny how the last two months had gently changed her perspective. Ever since Wes had made room for her in his life, her world had expanded to include new and wonderful feelings she'd never known could exist. Sometimes it was tough to separate herself from her fierce feelings of love for Wes at work. But never once had he said he loved her; and she had to bite back admitting it to him. Maggie was old enough to know that in a solid relationship, nothing could or should be forced from the other person. Wes had wanted more than a one-night stand from her, but anything long-term, like marriage, was out of the question. Yet, to her surprise,

Maggie was thinking about marriage for the first time in her life as something positive—not a pain in the rear or something expected of her because she was a woman.

With a sigh, Maggie leaned back and closed her eyes. *Red Flag.* Never had she been happier—or more frightened. She worried about her spotty flight performance. And she had to struggle with the fact that two days after Red Flag, Wes would be ordered back to the carrier for another three months until his enlistment was up. After that, he headed to UPS flight school to hone his skills on their jumbo jets.

Opening her eyes, Maggie stared straight ahead, feeling more than thinking. Over the past two months with Wes, her priorities had changed. She loved Wes, but he'd made it plain that his life was already mapped out. Marriage wasn't a part of his plans. Maggie herself was stuck in the Navy for another four years, and in spite of her recent problems, she couldn't imagine doing anything other than flying jets.

Rubbing her brow, Maggie grimaced. The thought of Wes leaving, walking out of her life forever, was piercing her heart with an overwhelming sadness that she didn't think she could survive. She'd never realized that love, real love, could be this exhilarating with joy at finding it—and just as pulverizing at the thought of losing it. Somehow she had to push her personal grief aside and remain focused on Red Flag. Somehow...

"Hell of a place," Wes remarked as they stood beside their F-14 on the ramp at Nellis Air Force Base,

Nevada. All around them, fighters, bombers and Aggressor F-5 jets were lined up. Tan-colored desert stretched into the distance, with odd clumps of mountains occasionally breaking the horizon. He forced his attention back to Maggie, who had grown more and more reclusive as they'd neared Nellis. Her lovely mouth had become a grim line revealing the tension and worry she suffered.

"Come on, Red," he urged softly. "Let's go over to Ops, check in and get our barracks assignment." With a smile, Wes added, "I'm going to miss having you in my arms at night."

Maggie forced a smile she didn't feel as they walked toward the dark blue van that would take them to Nellis Ops. "That's nice to hear."

"You'll be in my dreams every night, though."

Rallying at his teasing, Maggie finally laughed. "Okay, okay. I'll ease up. I'm just so damn nervous, I don't know what to do with myself." Looking over at the van, she saw that Dana and her RIO were already seated, waiting for them. Dana looked grim, too. So much was riding on their collective shoulders. They were the only women combat-pilots ever to take part in Red Flag. Already, Maggie could see the brazen or accusing stares aimed in their direction. Maggie was sure her and Dana's "fame" had preceded them.

"Listen, when we get over to Ops or the O club, don't take insults from some of these pilots personally," Wes warned her in a low tone. "There're going to be some guys who don't like you on their turf, Maggie. Just ride it out. Don't buy into it."

"I'm going to try, Wes. But my flight confidence isn't that strong, yet. I don't want to put myself on the firing line all over again with a jerk who acts like Brad Hall."

"Well," Wes said grimly, "any jock or RIO who starts to hassle you, I'll be there to put a stop to it pronto."

She smiled up at him, her heart swelling with such love that Maggie thought it might truly be possible to die from happiness. "For the first time in my life, I understand what it's like to be protected. It's a nice feeling, Wes."

The hot Nevada sun beat down on them. Wes had to control the urge to put his arm around Maggie's shoulders and hug her. Her flight confidence was still delicate—not as brittle as before, but still in the process of being rebuilt, brick by brick, in a new and better way. Wes anguished over the terrible stress that Red Flag would put on Maggie. Worse, he knew she and Dana were going to take a verbal beating on the ground from the jet jocks gathered at Nellis. It was going to be five days of hell in the air and hell on the ground. Could Maggie handle it? Could she pull from that deep source within herself and find the courage to keep going?

"Well, well—" a booming voice rolled out across the flight-desk area of Operations "—if it ain't the world-famous Lieutenant Donovan."

The ten pilots lounging around the counter, waiting to check in, all turned. Maggie felt heat rising in her cheeks as she and Wes moved up to the counter to file their flight plans. The officer who had hurled the attack was a Marine Corps pilot on the far end. Maggie met and held his dark blue gaze, although it was filled with animosity. She saw the patch on his flight suit. Captain Jace Larsen, USMC.

"Ignore him," Wes muttered.

Good advice. Maggie endured the collective stares as the talk at the counter sank into a stilted silence. When Dana and her RIO came up on the other side of Wes, Larsen spoke again.

"Navy must be hard up, having to send girls to do the work of men."

Anger got the better of Maggie. "Stow it, Larsen. Talk's cheap. Is that what you jarheads do on the ground—talk people to death? What counts is what we do in the air. Let's just see how well you do up there."

Dana grinned at Maggie. "Well put. I don't think I have anything to add," she said, glowering over at Larsen.

Larsen and his three Marine Corps pilot buddies glared back. "Hey, Donovan," he gloated. "You gonna lose another F-14? I hear you didn't like the paint job on your last one and decided to throw it away and shop around for a better color. Just like a woman: shopping and spending our hard-earned money."

Maggie bristled. Wes's hand clamped down on her shoulder in silent warning. She was allowing Larsen to get to her. Instantly, she relaxed and Wes let his hand drop from her shoulder. She ignored the pilot's comments, but the rest of the men at the counter, obviously aware that she'd lost a fighter, tittered nervously. The air was thick with tension.

Maggie endured another twenty minutes of staring as the pilots milled around. She was grateful for Wes's presence. When they'd finally checked in and gotten their barracks assignments, the four of them left Ops.

They took a van to the barracks officers' quarters. As they got out with their gear, Dana said, "I'm going to unpack and stay at the barracks."

"Don't you want to join us over at the O club for a cold drink?" Maggie asked, walking up the brick sidewalk.

"No, I'm going to rest up. You go ahead without me."

Maggie would be sharing a room with Dana at the BOQ. She looked up at Wes.

"See you in the foyer in about fifteen minutes?"

"Roger that."

Maggie entered the O club. She'd taken time for a quick, cooling shower and had changed into civilian clothes—a pair of wine-colored cotton slacks and a short-sleeved cotton shirt in a pink and white stripe. Her lightweight white sandals felt good after the bulky flight boots. Since many of the pilots coming and going in the busy O club assumed she was a groupie, she had to endure curious looks.

Wes wore a pair of light blue twill slacks and a gingham sport shirt with a white collar. In Maggie's eyes, he looked devastatingly handsome. He winked at her in the silent message of hello he always gave her when they were in a place where he couldn't otherwise show his affection.

Leaning over as he guided her into the noisy bar area, Wes whispered, "You outclass every lady here."

Maggie smiled. "You're full of malarkey, Bishop." But she loved him for his ability to help her relax, taking her mind off the constant tension she felt.

Wes, because of his height, was able to spot a lone table against the wall that wasn't occupied. The din of conversation warred with the jukebox playing favorites of the sixties. The low lighting, the clink of glasses, the hands waving in gestures showing airplanes in flight, the cigarette smoke—all combined to make it a typical O-club atmosphere, with jocks drinking beer— "aircrew debriefing fluid"—after their flights. The O club was the entertainment hub of any single pilot's life.

Maggie seated herself in the chair next to the wall while Wes took the chair closest to the constant bar traffic. A harried waitress finally made it over to their table, squeezing between clusters of pilots standing with beers in hand.

"Two lemonades," Wes ordered.

Maggie smiled at him after she'd left. "It's a good idea not to drink during Red Flag."

"Yeah," Wes agreed, stretching out his long legs beneath the table. "Alcohol and good reflexes don't mix." His eyes twinkled with devilry. "How are you doing?"

Before Maggie could respond, Captain Larsen and his fellow jocks emerged from the wall of green flight uniforms. Larsen's narrow face and close-set eyes reminded Maggie of a coyote. And she was obviously his next victim. Her eyes narrowed as he approached.

"Well, whaddya know, here's Donovan again. Hey, you look better in civvies, honey. Ya know, if ya don't make it as a combat pilot, you can always hustle your bustle over here. I'm sure some of these jocks wouldn't mind chasing you around. Whaddya think?"

Wes was out of his chair like a huge spring unwinding. In one fluid motion, he turned, gripped Larsen by the shoulders of his flight suit and gave him a good, solid jerk that made his head and neck snap back.

"I think," Wes whispered tautly between clenched teeth, "that you'd better go peddle your garbage somewhere else, Larsen."

"Hey," another Marine pilot growled, gripping Wes by the shoulder, "lay off, Navy puke."

Maggie was out of her chair in an instant. "Knock it off!" she snarled at all of them, her eyes blazing with fury. "Who do you think you are? Let go of my RIO, mister, or I'll let you have it right between the running lights."

Wes watched the Marine pilot jump back, his eyes wide with shock. He swallowed a grin. Maggie stood, furious, her hands on her hips. She rounded on Larsen. Wes let go of him.

"And you, Larsen. I'm ashamed of you! As a fellow officer, we're taught to be polite and respectful. Especially to other officers!" She punched him in the chest with her finger, her face mere inches from his. "Anything you got to say to me, you say up in the air. I understand the Marines and Air Force contingents are going to be the aggressors, while the Army and

Navy represent U.S. forces. You're my enemy, Larsen. Come and get me in the air, and we'll just see what you're made of, mister.''

Larsen took a step back, jerking the front of his flight suit back into place. The bar had quieted considerably; everyone's attention zeroed in on them. His lips drew back in a snarl. ''Okay, honey, you got a deal. For the next five days I'm gonna be on your six every time you think you're safe. I'm gonna wipe your tail all over the Nellis sky. No woman can fly combat.''

Her nostrils flaring, Maggie stood her ground, shaking with anger. ''You'd better believe it, Larsen. And I don't let anyone on my six. Especially some swelled-headed jerk from the Marine Corps who thinks he's hot in the clench.''

Wes gripped Maggie's arm, afraid the confrontation would escalate. He wouldn't put it past Larsen to take a swing at Maggie if she pushed him too far.

''Come on, Maggie, let's go.''

Maggie resisted, but Wes persevered, and finally she backed off. Her glare at Larsen never wavered. Nor did his.

''See you in the air bright and early tomorrow morning,'' Larsen taunted her in a loud voice. ''You're dead meat, Donovan. Dead meat!''

Once out in the hot, dry afternoon air, Wes released Maggie's arm. They walked down the sidewalk toward the curb where they would wait to catch one of the frequent vans that acted as buses on base.

''Were you really going to hit that guy between the running lights?'' he wanted to know.

Maggie muttered a curse as she stood tapping her foot. "Of course not! I've never hit anyone in my whole life. But I'll tell you what, Wes, if I ever considered it, Larsen would be the first. That guy's rabid!"

Chuckling, Wes nodded. "Do you know how pretty you look when you're angry?" Then he quickly held up both hands in a gesture of peace as her eyes got huge. "I was just kidding!"

"I'm so mad right now, Wes, I could spit! I won't take those kinds of slurs sitting down."

"I know. That's why I got up first and nailed Larsen," he said dryly, watching a van round the block and come toward them.

"Thanks for stepping in. Usually I have to protect myself."

The need to kiss Maggie, to hold her in his arms, was building into an ache deep in Wes. "One of the many nice things about a relationship is that partners can protect each other," he reminded her.

Maggie softened beneath his whispered words. "I like what we have, Wes."

The bus came to a stop and the doors opened. "So do I," he agreed, his voice filled with feeling. As they boarded, Wes's mind was on other things. Maggie had made an enemy of Larsen. Whether she knew it or not, he was going to make her life miserable in the air—a threat she hadn't counted on. Could Maggie endure the added pressure of Larsen's savagery?

Chapter Eleven

"Maggie, our target is Quarzite West on Range 75," Wes reported, his eyes constantly roving across his radars for a first warning of approaching aircraft or SAM missiles. They flew with three Navy Tomcats and four Army fighters. Maggie was leading the wing.

"Roger." She kept rubbernecking around. Somewhere in the cloudless blue morning sky, either above or below them, lurked the aggressors, waiting to shoot them down and engage them in dogfights. More than anything, Maggie knew Larsen would be hunting her in earnest in his F-14 Tomcat.

Range 75 was a forward resupply point and second-echelon target in the Gold Flat area of Nellis where today's scenario was to be played out. The planes representing U.S. forces were to make a bombing run, drop their loads and get out cleanly. The problem was the SAM missile sites that ringed the bombing-run area. Maggie was sweating.

The brown desert earth became a blur as Maggie led her team of eight jets down between the barren mountains. Ahead of her was Gold Flat, a piece of real estate that looked like Kansas: flat as a pancake.

Wes kept up his chatter, constantly checking his radars and then the sky around them. The mountains on either side of them were potentially lethal when they initiated their bombing run. The aggressors could be flying two or three hundred feet off the nap of the earth, and he wouldn't be able to detect them with his instruments. Only their alertness and their eyes could give them any kind of warning if the aggressors were indeed "hiding" behind the mountains, waiting for just the right moment to leap them from the rear—on their "six"—and shoot them down electronically.

"We'll take the first run." Maggie signaled the other planes. She eyed the mountains warily. "Wes, I got an ugly feeling Larsen and his boys are hiding behind those hills."

"Roger that. Nothing on radar."

"Roger. Keep your eyes peeled."

"You got it."

Guiding the Tomcat to a specific point at the end of the flat, Maggie listened to Wes's navigation instructions. He was her bombardier-navigator, as well as her radar specialist. She honed in on his orders, as the jet howled along at four hundred miles an hour, right on the beam to drop the electronic load of bombs.

Just as she got ready to "pickle," or trigger, the bombs, a warning shriek indicated that an aggressor had her jet in its gunsights.

Jerking a look behind, Maggie saw an F-14 looming up fast on her rear.

"Bogey eight o'clock! Bank right!" Wes yelled.

The bombing run had to wait. Maggie heard Dana, her wingwoman, screaming in her headset.

"I'm on him! I'm on him! Stay on target!"

Sweating heavily, Maggie held the Tomcat steady. The warning continued to scream that any second now the aggressor would fire an electronic missile and kill them. *Hurry, Dana! Shoot the bastard!*

"Steady, steady," Wes crooned, his breathing ragged. "Now! Pickle them now!"

Savagely pressing the button on the stick, Maggie pulled the fighter up, shoving the throttles forward to afterburner range. The F-14 leaped skyward in a howl of thunderous power. Craning to one side, Maggie saw that Dana had scared the aggressor off her tail. Was it Larsen? It had to be! Now it was her turn to protect Dana on her bomb run.

For the next hour above Gold Flat, Maggie engaged in a series of hotly contested dogfights. If a fighter was "shot down" electronically, by gentleman's agreement, that fighter had to return to base and leave the fray. When the fighting was all over, Maggie had been shot down by one of the two remaining Marine Corps F-14s. She didn't know whose. They returned to base.

Back at debriefing, Maggie sat with a Pepsi in hand, dying of thirst. She felt washed out by the demanding

G's and stress of combat, the first time she'd gotten a real taste of what it would be like to engage an enemy as skilled as she. Wes sat next to her. Dana and her RIO were seated farther down the line of chairs.

Larsen swaggered into the debriefing, still wearing his G-suit and carrying his duffel bag. He nailed Maggie with a grin and cocked his hand like a gun.

"Bang. You're dead, Lieutenant Donovan. I just wanted to let you know I was the one that bagged you out there."

"Took you almost an hour to do it, Larsen. I wouldn't be bragging too much. The boys over at the O club will say you were slow on the draw."

Larsen's smile disappeared. "I got you, Donovan. And I'll get you every day. You're gonna be number sixteen on the list at the end of this five-day course. No woman can be a combat pilot."

Maggie held on to her disintegrating temper. Wes gave her a silent warning that spoke volumes, and she remained slouched in her chair, seething silently.

The debrief officer for the Gold Flats scenario came in. Not only was their flight electronically videotaped by Nellis officials, but special gun cameras in the aggressor aircraft also recorded the dogfights. Between the two, Maggie knew that fewer pilots would lie about getting "shot down." Still, when it came down to basics, there were situations where a pilot's word had to carry the day.

Wes leaned over, whispering, "I'm going to look forward to the film from Larsen's camera to see if he did get us."

"I don't think he did," Maggie growled under her breath, watching the cocky fighter-pilot sit down in a chair opposite them.

"Even if he did," Wes told her quietly, "you performed beautifully, Maggie. You did so many other things right for a rookie combat pilot. Look at those Army guys. They got shot down and had to return to base in the first fifteen minutes after the aggressors leaped us."

She nodded. As usual, Wes was right, and she took some hope from his words. The debrief officer, Major Lars Anderson, stood behind a podium next to a huge screen that would show every second of their air engagement over Gold Flats. Maggie broke into another sweat, trading glances with Dana, who had not been shot down during the fray.

"Not bad for a first time," Wes congratulated Maggie as they chose to walk back from Ops toward the BOQ, ten blocks away.

Maggie gave him a disgruntled look. "What? Getting nailed by Larsen? God, I was embarrassed. He caught me in such a rookie position. I should have known better. I should have—"

"You shot down three planes, Maggie. Two more and you'd have been an ace on your first day of Red Flag." Wes grinned, proud as hell of her. She looked strained and drawn, with little color in her face. Her hair, formerly brushed and shining, was mussed, giving her a little-girl look. Once again, Wes found himself wishing they were alone, so he could hold her. He knew how much that helped Maggie—and it helped him, too. It wasn't a one-way street. Real love never was.

"I know," Maggie murmured, walking slowly at his side, her hands deep in the pockets of her flight suit. "Dana did really well."

"Dana doesn't have Larsen hunting her, either."

"I suppose not."

The afternoon sun was hot and dry. Wes lifted his head. Planes were continually landing and taking off from the busy military base. The rumble of jets echoed across the huge, sprawling installation. "Hey, would you like to drive into Vegas and have a nice dinner? A little dancing?"

"No... I don't think so. I want to go over what happened up there today, Wes. I'm not making the same mistake twice."

"Maggie, don't get tunnel vision on this. You know what happens when you do."

"I know." She tried to smile, but failed. "Can I take a rain check on your dinner?"

"Anytime, Red. Anytime."

They walked in silence for a couple of blocks. Maggie noticed the base housing off in the distance. They were one-story stucco homes painted ivory or white to discourage the heat of the sun. The yards were green and brown, but neatly kept, and flowers struggled beneath the hundred-degree heat that was common for the area during the summer and fall months. She saw children playing and some of the wives out at the fences, chatting. The children reminded her of Molly.

"I think I'm going to call Molly and see how she's doing. She's so miserable now."

"Good idea," Wes agreed. "Rachel's a big kid. Probably going to be a ten-pounder when she finally decides to be born."

"I just hope Cam pulls in to port in time to be with Molly. She wants that so badly. We all do."

"I'd give my right arm to be there, too," Wes said, meaning it. He brightened. "Let's hope Molly holds off for you two gals to fly back to be her coaches."

Some of Maggie's depression lifted. "Roger that."

At BOQ they separated, going to different floors. In her room, Maggie sat down on the narrow bunk and rubbed her face. She was completely washed out. Unlacing her flight boots, she stretched out and closed her eyes. Having barely been able to sleep at all the week before Red Flag, Maggie knew that exhaustion was one of her many problems. But tomorrow was another day. Another chance to improve her rating. Right now, she stood number six out of sixteen. More than anything, she wanted to be number one—to prove to herself that she had regained all that she'd lost in the crash.

Just as Maggie put her foot on the ladder to climb into the F-14 cockpit, she heard Larsen's voice behind her.

"You're mine today, Donovan."

Maggie tossed a look over her shoulder at the pilot. "Like hell we are."

He grinned and tossed her a mock salute. "See you over Pahute Mesa, Lieutenant."

Wes glared at the Marine as he swaggered on by, walking down the line of fighter aircraft and crews getting ready for the next day of battle.

"He's a real pain, isn't he?"

Maggie mounted the ladder, feeling shaky inside. "Yeah."

Once in the rear seat, Wes plugged in the intercom jack. "Maggie, you read me?" She had just fitted her helmet on her head.

"Loud and clear."

"Did you get some sleep last night?"

Maggie allowed Chantal to help her strap into the harnesses. "Yes, some. You?"

"Slept like a baby."

"You would."

"I just dreamed I had you in my arms, that's all."

She grinned and thanked Chantal, who climbed back down the ladder. Out of earshot of her crew, Maggie said, "I missed you, too."

"How much?"

"Much."

Wes busied himself with preflight, checking his scopes and the other instruments in front of him. "I like the sound of your voice when you talk about us, Red. It gets low and husky, like warm brandy flowing over me."

"You're such a romantic. You're as bad as Molly."

"But you love it."

Yes, she did love him. Maggie bit down hard on her lip. Already, this was the second day of Red Flag. Wes was supposed to leave for carrier duty two days after his return to Miramar. The days were slipping by too quickly.

"I wish we didn't have to sleep in barracks," Maggie complained.

The canopy slowly lowered over them and Wes saw Maggie give her crew a thumbs-up. They were ready for taxi. Having waited for an opportunity when she wouldn't be busy, Wes finally pushed the intercom as they were slowly moving out toward the runway.

"You know we don't have to stay on board the base."

"What are you talking about?"

"We could slip off base after these flights, get a hotel room and stay with each other every night."

The idea was tantalizing to Maggie. The F-14 bobbed up and down as it rode across depressions in the surface of the concrete. "Do you think we'd be discovered?" Although it wasn't against regulations, Maggie didn't want her image tarnished—not for herself, but for what she symbolized to other women. She was terribly conscious of how her own personal behavior could be blown out of proportion by the hounding press or male pilots.

"I think, if we're prudent and plan it, no one will be the wiser." Wes wanted to talk Maggie into the idea, but he knew she'd have to make up her own mind on this.

"Let me think about it, okay?"

"Okay, Red. Well, let's turn and burn. I've got a feeling Larsen and his aggressor squadron are going to zero in on us to finish us off early today."

"Not if we can help it," Maggie replied through gritted teeth.

Flying at thirty-four thousand feet, Maggie was now number four in the slot of the U.S. squadron. The Army was taking their turn today at being leaders. Today, their object was to find tanks and destroy them electronically.

Maggie was sweating heavily in the cockpit, jumpy and continually rubbernecking around.

"I feel him," she told Wes. "I feel that bastard Larsen somewhere around me. I swear I can."

"He's not on my scopes, Maggie." Wes frowned, craning his neck, slitting his eyes against the blinding glare of the sun. In air-combat terms, the fighter to come *out* of the sun toward his enemy had the best chance of a kill. Would Larsen and his bunch be up above them? Until the aggressors turned on their own radar scopes, which Wes could instantly pick up, they could sneak up on them. Again, only sharp eyes could save them from being caught off guard.

Maggie heard the Army call for the wing to make a long, banking turn to the left to one thousand feet. Seconds later, the hair stood up on the back of her neck.

"Bogey at three-five-nine!" Wes barked.

Too late! An F-14 fighter flashed yards in front of Maggie's craft. It was Larsen! Instantly, both her engines went into a compressor stall as she hit the turbulent air.

Maggie's eyes bulged. The Tomcat fought her violently as it began a slow arc downward. Her hands moving at lightning speed, she stop-cocked the throttles. If she couldn't get at least one engine restarted, they would have to eject! Not again! Not again! her mind shrieked at her.

"Compressor stalls!" Wes gasped.

"I've got it!" Maggie responded instantly in a strangled tone. Wes could do nothing except wait helplessly.

The fighter wouldn't glide very long. Larsen had deliberately flown too close to cause the problem. That was against regulations! Anger mixed with overwhelming fear as Maggie felt the G's building up against her. Negative G's were always a bitch, punching and draining her, making every hand movement a superhuman effort.

"Mayday, Mayday," Wes began to radio. "This is Red Dog Four. We've got a twin compressor stall..."

Maggie blotted out the rest of what Wes was doing, all her focus on the instrument panel before her. Blips of the eagle smashing into the canopy struck at her. Sweat beaded and fell into her eyes, making them smart. She had to get one engine started! At least one! Teeth clenched, straining to breathe against the G's building up, she set the throttle for the port engine. Pressing the button, she prayed it would restart.

"Come on, come on!"

The seconds unwound. The altimeter was speeding up, the little arm whirling round and round. They were at twenty thousand feet. If she couldn't get the aircraft under control by fifteen thousand, by regulations they *had* to eject.

"Maggie—"

"I'm trying!"

Suddenly, the dials for the port engine rumbled to life. The engine had restarted! Relief shattered through Maggie. The F-14 sluggishly responded to her command and slowed the dive earthward. Maggie applied strong right rudder to put the plane on straight, level flight.

Sucking in huge drafts of oxygen, Maggie tried restart for the starboard engine. Nothing happened. Three times she tried, but the engine refused to start.

"No go," she reported to Wes. "Call base and tell them we're returning with an in-flight emergency and get us immediate clearance. I've got only one engine working."

"Roger." Wes drew in a deep, ragged breath of air. Anger roiled through him after he made the call. Because of the in-flight emergency, they would automatically be cleared to land and taken out of the day's planned events.

Landing was easy. Maggie brought the F-14 down on the concrete runway, popping the speed brakes on the wings as soon as touchdown occurred. On the way back to the ramp, she finally began to relax.

"It was that bastard Larsen that flew in front of us," Maggie said angrily. "I'm reporting him for this!"

"I'll do it," Wes told her grimly.

"He could've killed us!"

"I don't think that was his intention," Wes said. "I think he wanted to shake you up, make you lose it."

"All he's done is rile me! I'm going to hang him by his rear!"

* * *

Maggie seethed for the rest of the day. They filed a protest at Ops after landing. Wes decided the wisest thing to do was to get Maggie off base to cool down before she took Larsen apart piece by piece after he landed at noontime. Wes practically had to drag her out of Ops and over to the BOQ to change into civilian clothes.

After they'd reached Las Vegas by bus, Wes chose a Chinese restaurant for their late lunch. Maggie sat beside him, tense and still so angry, he knew that silence was the better part of valor.

Over Oolong tea, halfway through their meal in the darkened, quiet of the restaurant, Maggie finally calmed down. She gave Wes a slight smile.

"I've never been so peeved before."

"I can tell." He smiled and poured her more tea. "Under the circumstances, you handled the emergency perfectly. Congratulations."

Wes always made her feel good about herself. "What would I do without you around?"

His smile broadened. "Pine away for me, Maggie Donovan. You'll die of loneliness if I don't hang around to keep reminding you that you're one hell of a woman and pilot."

His smile drove straight through her heart, and Maggie felt humbled by the love she saw in his eyes. But each of them knew that very shortly he would be gone—gone and out of her life. "Well," she whispered, idly moving the fork through the noodles on her plate, "things just won't be the same without you around, Wes." Her world would be bleak and gray.

"Then let's make the most of what's left, Maggie. Let's take a room here at one of the big hotels. No one is going to know. The only one who might care is Larsen, and chances are, he's so worried about you jumping him back on base, he's not going to be hanging around you from now on. Not after what he pulled."

She nodded. "Okay, let's do it. I really miss sleeping with you at night."

He grinned.

"Oh, stop it. You've got that smile like I can't live without you, Bishop. Men think they're so indispensable to women," she grouched good-naturedly.

Relieved that Maggie was finally over her anger, Wes laughed heartily. How fiercely he loved her and all her intense moods. "I hope I'm a *little* indispensable to you," he baited.

"You know you are, Bishop, so quit fishing for compliments. Come on, hurry up and finish eating. I want to be in your arms. I want to love you."

"I always said you were my dessert, Red."

Dana stood looking at the tally of totals on the bulletin board just outside the main auditorium where the pilots met every morning for a briefing before each flight. Maggie stood at her shoulder.

"We're looking good," Dana said. "Out of sixteen, I'm number six and you're number four." She flashed a smile over at her friend. "Not bad for two women, huh?"

"Not bad at all," Wes congratulated them, coming up and standing beside Maggie. He handed both women a cup of coffee.

Looking around, Maggie didn't see Larsen. Since the incident on Tuesday, he'd kept a really low profile. One reason was that the Ops officer knocked him down two points in the overall standings for his ploy to scare her out of the air. Larsen was now rated number five. That did Maggie's heart good.

"Last day," Maggie told them. There was sadness in her tone. It was the last day for a lot of things. Last day of Red Flag, which had been an incredible learning experience. Maggie's confidence was stronger than ever. It was the last day in the cockpit with Wes. By this afternoon, they'd wrap up Red Flag and fly back to Miramar. On Sunday, he was due to take a flight out to Hawaii, and then to Okinawa to meet up with his carrier. She was so glad they'd decided to spend their nights together at the hotel instead of staying at Nellis. So glad.

"Today, I'm going to get Larsen if it's the last thing I do," Maggie warned Wes on the way to their fighter, which was parked on the ramp. The morning was dawning clear and cloudless, as usual. The air was crisp, and Maggie inhaled it deeply.

"We're supposed to fly over Tolicha Peak and bomb the imaginary industrial complex, airfield and railroad, Maggie. I don't think we're going to have much time or fuel to do anything else. And we've got surface to air missile sights to avoid, ringing that entire area. It's a bitch of a test without trying to even the score with Larsen."

"I don't care," she said tightly, halting at the ladder. "I want you to watch for the bastard. If I see him, I'm taking him out."

Wes understood Maggie's need to get even with Larsen, but patiently he told her, "First objective is the bombings, okay?"

Maggie refused to respond.

"Maggie?"

"Oh, all right. I'll finish the bombings. But I'm warning you, Wes, if I see Larsen, we're going after him."

"Fine by me. Let's mount up."

There was no way to prepare adequately for the fifth day, in Maggie's opinion. Not only were there aggressor aircraft, but an extra squadron of F-5s, also aggressors, were in the air. Their flight of eight friendly aircraft was outgunned two to one. It didn't matter.

Maggie was careful how much fuel she expended on the way to the target. After the bombing runs had been successfully completed, she went after Larsen. It was easy to pick out the twin tail of his F-14. She knew it too well. Dana, her wingwoman, hung close, knowing what Maggie was going to do.

The sky above Tolicha Peak suddenly became the stage for a deadly ballet in the air. Larsen took immediate evasive action when Maggie had locked onto his tail. The warning scream of her missiles locking onto his aircraft sounded in her helmet.

"I've got him, I've got him!" Maggie cried triumphantly. His afterburners lit, Larsen was a thousand feet below her and trying to twist from side to side to get out of her missile range.

"Easy!" Wes warned. The F-14 bucked and danced all over the sky as Maggie honed in on Larsen.

"Damn!" The buzzer stopped sounding. Maggie watched as Larsen did a split-second maneuver and effectively escaped her. Not for long! She shoved the throttles to the firewall, her fingers tight over them. Larsen was going to try and shoot straight up, gain altitude on her, make a roll and come down on her six to shoot her instead.

"No way, you bastard," she snarled softly, the G's building as she pushed the Tomcat straight up, matching Larsen's movement. In moments, the two fighters were parallel, within five hundred feet of each other. Maggie looked over. She could see Larsen's helmeted head. He flipped his middle finger at her.

Maggie held on to her temper. She knew Larsen was trying to get her angry enough to make a stupid error. No way! Not now. The F-14 continued to strain upward, its engines screaming. Soon, Maggie knew, they'd run out of altitude and power at the same time. What to do? If she peeled off first, Larsen would have her in his gunsights within seconds, and she'd be dead.

"You'd better do something fast," Wes warned her with a grunt as the G's pounded him.

"I will!" Suddenly Maggie jerked back the lever. The air brakes on both wings dropped, slowing the fighter considerably. Larsen's F-14 flashed ahead. She jammed the throttles forward to afterburner range, jerking the air brakes up to allow the fighter to leap forward.

"Aha! I got you now, you bastard!" And indeed Maggie had. The scream of her missiles filled her head. But she was too close to fire a missile and quickly switched the selector to Guns. Thumbing the button, the electronic beep indicating hits on Larsen's aircraft began pinging in her ears. It was music to Maggie's ears.

"You're dead, Larsen!" she shouted triumphantly over the radio.

The other pilot was supposed to acknowledge.

Maggie hung on Larsen's tail and continued to pummel him with electronic hits. "Larsen, acknowledge you're hit!"

"No way!"

Maggie watched Larsen bank to the right. She wrenched the stick in the same direction. "Okay, you cheater, I'll show you." Allowing Larsen to get about a mile ahead of her, Maggie switched to her Sparrow missiles. She knew that Ops would be able to electronically confirm her "kill" this way. With guns, they couldn't.

"Stay on him, Maggie. Stay on him," Wes crooned. "You've got 'em, you've got 'em...."

Savagely jamming down the button on her stick, with Larsen's aircraft within the "kill" circle of her HUD, she watched in great satisfaction as one of her two missiles struck Larsen's F-14.

"You're dead, Larsen," Maggie radioed him sweetly. "Shot down by a woman who isn't supposed to be able to be a combat pilot. What are you going to tell your buddies back home, huh?" She laughed.

Wes grinned and shook his head. That was his Maggie. Larsen would never live this down. It was a good way to get even with the Marine. Wes's smile disappeared as they headed back to base, the mission a complete success. What was he going to do? Just walk out of Maggie's life in two more days? What the hell was he going to do?

Chapter Twelve

"Maggie! Maggie!"

Dana's voice carried down the hall of BOQ and Maggie opened the door. Dana came to a halt, breathing raggedly. Her eyes were huge.

"I just got a phone call. Guess what? Griff and Cam are in port!" She grinned. "And Molly's gone into labor!"

"Oh, my God," Maggie whispered. "When? How long ago?"

Dana could barely stand still. "Cam called her from the carrier as it was pulling into San Diego harbor, and I guess she went into labor. Isn't that crazy? Isn't that wonderful? I'll get to see Griff! And Cam will be here for the birth of his baby!"

Maggie hugged Dana. "I'm so happy for you. I know how much you missed him."

"We've got to pack and get out of here. We've got to call our crews and tell them to ready our planes—"

Laughing, Maggie said, "Slow down, Dana. I've never seen you like this before."

Dana pulled her small suitcase out from beneath her bunk. "I haven't been separated from my husband for six months before, either."

Someone had to keep a semblance of calm around here, Maggie decided. "What about Molly? How long does labor last?"

Shrugging, Dana jerked open the drawer of the dresser that stood next to her bunk. "You went to Molly's classes, too. She's just started. I'm sure we've got time."

Despite the need for calm, Maggie found herself getting excited. "Well, is Dr. Ruth Culver there? And Molly's midwife, Karen?"

"Yes," Dana answered. "Molly's already called them. Ruth is coming over right away, and Karen's finishing a midwife detail for a woman up in Bonsall. She said she'd be with Molly in about two hours." Flashing her an enthusiastic smile, Dana called over her shoulder, "Don't worry, Maggie. Now, all of a sudden, you're acting like a nervous mother-to-be, yourself."

"Yeah, maybe I am." Maggie pulled her bag out from beneath her bunk. "I want to get ahold of Wes. He's got a vested interest in Molly's baby, too."

"Doesn't he, though?" Dana straightened and turned. "You know, if I hadn't seen it with my own eyes, I'd never have believed it."

"What?" Maggie stood poised over the phone.

"Cam's wife and child were killed in an airline crash a year before he met Molly. He's a real family-oriented guy. I just never thought men got that excited or involved in a woman having a baby, that's all. Wes is just as excited as Cam is. Maybe I'm out of touch. I don't know."

"Look at Wes. He wasn't there for the birth of his daughter, Annie, and he still feels that deeply."

"Kinda like a wound that hasn't healed," Dana ventured softly.

"Exactly." And then Maggie shook her head. "Isn't it something? The birth of a child can pull so many people together? Cam's walking on air and chomping at the bit to get permission to leave the carrier. And I'll bet Wes is going to be excited in his own way. After Molly let him feel Rachel kicking, he's been like a doting uncle around her."

"I think," Maggie added, feeling a wall of emotion expand her heart, "that Wes needs to be there. I think if he is, if Molly doesn't mind, this birth will be a healing experience for him, too."

"Putting a lot of ghosts to rest," Dana added. She sighed and shook her head. "What a crazy, messed-up world we live in, isn't it? We know two men who love their families and children more than most. I just never would have believed it."

"That's because your father abandoned you and your mother."

"That's all over," Dana whispered. "Being married to Griff these last two wonderful years has taught me a lot about the good in men. I still don't trust most of them, but he's helping me get over that."

"Better watch it, Dana, or you'll be telling me you're pregnant, too," she teased.

With a shrug, Dana went back to packing. "I'm not ready for that step yet, Maggie. Maybe in the future. Near thirty feels right to me. What about you?"

"Me?"

"Is there an echo in here?"

Grinning, Maggie picked up the phone and called over to the hangar. The entire Navy team would leave in two hours. Setting the receiver back in the cradle, Maggie was about to leave to find Wes when Dana stopped her.

"You never answered my question, Maggie. What about you and Wes? You two are inseparable."

Sitting down on her bunk, Maggie folded her hands between her legs and stared down at the polished wooden floor. "I don't know, Dana."

"Don't give me that."

"I don't know."

"Do you love the guy?"

Maggie shrugged. "Even if I said yes, it doesn't matter." Glancing up at Dana as she wandered over to her bunk, Maggie tried to cheer up. "You and Molly get the thing you most wanted back in the world: your husbands. And Cam gets the baby he's needed for so long. Everyone gets something good."

Sitting down, Dana put her arm around Maggie's shoulders. "And you lose out because Wes leaves for his carrier this Sunday."

Maggie tried to shrug it off. "Life goes on, doesn't it? On the flip side, in overall points, the Navy team has taken first place in the Red Flag competition. All four of us ended up in the top ten."

"You were highest. Number three. That isn't bad, Maggie."

"No," she whispered. "But it sure as hell takes the booby prize every time I think about Wes leaving."

Dana nodded somberly. "Molly and I have noticed a big change in you since Wes walked into your life."

"Oh?"

"Yeah, you're softer—you're more interested in other things in life besides flying."

"Wes did that. His 'playtime' as he calls it." She managed a short laugh. There was a silence in the room. Finally she whispered hoarsely, "Dana, I don't know what I'm going to do when he leaves. When I look back over the last three months, it's like he's become a permanent part of my life—how I see life and live it now. Wes was right: I was living in a tunnel of sorts before he came along. All I could see, taste, hear, smell and want was flying."

Patting her, Dana said, "The right person in your life enlarges everything for you, Maggie. Griff's certainly done that for me. But I've done it for him, too. It's a pretty awesome thing, how love can influence and broaden both people." She smiled over at her distraught friend. "More than anything, Griff has given me the courage not to be as afraid to open up and trust."

"Well," Maggie grumped, "you certainly had reason to distrust men after the way your father abused you."

"What I'm trying to say, Maggie, is that you're scared. You love Wes and he loves you. And don't go giving me that round-eyed look of yours. Molly and I figured it out two days after you met the guy. Have you told him you love him?"

"Not exactly...."

"You either have or you haven't."

"Okay, I haven't! But he hasn't, either."

"You're both scared," Dana pronounced confidently. She gave Maggie one more hug and then stood. "Are you just going to let him walk out of your life?"

"I don't know...."

"Maggie Donovan, I'm ashamed of you! Where's the infamous Celtic courage you've shown in every other department of your life? You're always bragging how it's gotten you through every scrape. Has it deserted you now?"

Maggie couldn't even be angry about Dana's fierce prodding. "You're right," she said glumly, resting her chin in the palm of her hand. "I've discovered I'm an absolute coward when it comes to personal relationships."

With a groan, Dana gripped Maggie by the shoulders and gave her a good shake. "You nitwit! Love makes us vulnerable. It makes us feel better than we ever felt. And it makes us feel more frightened than we ever thought possible because we're afraid to lose what's been given us. It's a gift, Maggie. The most beautiful gift in the world. Don't let fear stop you from being honest with Wes. The poor guy's probably just as scared as you are. He's probably afraid you'll turn him down if he admits he loves you.''

''I wouldn't do that.''

''*You* know that,'' Dana gloated, ''but *he* doesn't. Maggie, risk everything, will you? When you get a chance, take Wes aside after Molly has had her baby, and talk with him. Lay all the cards on the table.''

She grimaced. ''That's a hell of a gamble.''

''And what do you have to lose by doing it? You have everything to lose if you don't!''

With a nod, Maggie whispered, ''Okay, I'll talk to him.''

''Great!'' Dana released her and looked at her watch. ''Just think, in five hours we'll be home. Molly's in labor. I'll get to kiss my husband!'' She threw up her arms and whirled around, laughing. ''I can hardly wait!''

Maggie got up, smiling. In her heart, she felt no one deserved happiness more than Dana, because of her terrible childhood. With Griff's love and patience, Dana was blossoming. All because of love, Maggie mused. She left and went to find Wes. He wasn't in his room, and the clerk at the main desk said he'd seen him going down to the basement poolroom.

She found Wes alone in the large walnut-paneled room at one of the four pool tables.

''Hi,'' he greeted, leaning over and taking a shot at the black eight-ball. Maggie looked tired but happy. Wes tendered the desire to stop what he was doing, pull her into his arms and kiss her until she melted like hot fire against him. His loins automatically tightened at that searing thought.

Maggie halted near the table, running her fingers along its polished wooden edge. "Hi. Dana just told me some great news." When she finished by mentioning Molly going into labor, Wes's face lit up with genuine excitement. He put the pool cue aside and came around the table.

"Well, shouldn't we be flying back, then?"

Maggie smiled up at him, though anguish jagged through her. In two days she wouldn't be able to absorb his dancing blue eyes, that careless smile or the deep, resonant voice any longer. Wes would be gone. "It's all set up. We'll be leaving at 1300. You're going to have to hurry and pack."

Rubbing his hands together, Wes said, "No problem. Tell me about Molly. How's she doing?"

Walking up the stairs with him, Maggie filled him in on the details. Every time she thought about leveling with Wes about her love for him, fear shot through her. Maggie was ashamed of herself. With Wes's support, she'd gotten over her first failure. Was she going to fail at this, too? At admitting her love to him? Suddenly, Maggie felt more desperate than she ever had in her entire life, caught in a web that she felt would entrap her to the point where she would lose her ability to speak honestly to Wes about her feelings. Perhaps, after Molly gave birth, she would do it. She *had* to.

* * *

Upon landing at Miramar as the sun was setting over the Pacific Ocean, Dana went with Maggie to their locker room at Ops. They both took hot showers and changed into civilian clothes they kept in their lockers.

As Maggie pulled on the white cotton slacks and soft voile blouse of pale green, she saw Dana's eagerness to get over to Molly's. Her husband was waiting for her. Again, Maggie was struck by how much happiness love could bring to a person. Joy shone in Dana's eyes as she quickly ran a brush through her short black hair. She looked pretty in a cotton summer dress. The floral print brought out the stain of pink in her cheeks. In Maggie's eyes, Dana was exquisitely feminine in contrast with herself. Realizing she was depressed, Maggie tried not to be hard on herself or make comparisons. That was a dangerous combination.

Dana lifted her hand. "I gotta run! I'll see you over there soon?"

"Yes. Wes will drive me over as soon as he gets done showering and dressing. We won't be long. Tell Molly to hang in there."

Dana waved and disappeared out the door. Maggie stood in the locker room and looked around. Outside, the familiar sounds of jets taking off and landing could be heard. A terrible weight settled upon her. All the way back to Miramar, Wes had kept up a congenial chatter on the cockpit intercom, without any sign that he was sad to be leaving, or would miss her.

With a grimace, Maggie slipped the strap of her white purse over her left shoulder. First things first. Molly was in labor. It was a time for celebration, and Maggie desperately wanted to lose herself in the joyous occasion.

Wes was able to stay in the background once they got to Molly and Cam's home, and be a spectator of sorts. He immediately liked Cam, who was still dressed in his dark blue Navy uniform. With Griff Turcotte, it was a reunion composed of backslapping, handshaking and old stories. The apartment throbbed with subdued excitement. Cam was in the bedroom with his wife most of the time, along with the woman doctor and midwife.

Wes volunteered with Maggie to work in the kitchen, keeping a fresh pot of coffee on, making sandwiches for the two hungry pilots who had arrived minutes earlier from the carrier, and keeping Miracle, the dog, company. The black Lab was whining a great deal because she was used to sleeping at the foot of Molly's bed, but had been asked to leave during the birthing.

Maggie divided her time between being with Molly, as part of her labor team, and going into the living room to give Griff and Wes updates. There was such happiness swirling around the apartment that Maggie was no longer aware of her own underlying misery. Just seeing the enthusiasm in the faces of the men humbled Maggie. They were no less involved, no less excited than the women about the birth.

Perhaps more than anything, Maggie found herself on the verge of crying every time she went into the bedroom. Cam refused to leave his wife's side, sitting beside her, gently sponging off her face and arms with a cloth, talking soothingly to her as the contractions became more pronounced, and supporting her in touching ways. Maggie often sat in the rocker near the bed, stealing glances at them from time to time, feeling like a thief invading their privacy.

Every once in a while, Cam would lean over, kiss Molly's dry, chapped lips and whisper words to ease the pain that Maggie saw in her face. His tenderness toward Molly made Maggie's heart grow soft with such an array of emotions that she had to get up and leave the room. Why was she feeling this way? Moving to the kitchen to be alone, Maggie stood at the drain board, looking out the window at the small, fenced backyard.

"Are you all right?" Wes asked, coming up quietly behind her and slipping his hand across her shoulder. Maggie looked stricken.

Wes's hand sent a shaft of longing so incredibly deep through Maggie that words escaped her. Finally she nodded. "Yes . . . I'm fine."

"You look shaken."

"Just the excitement, I guess." How much Maggie wanted to turn around, seek Wes's arms and blurt out her feelings. But what good would it do? He'd be gone in two days, anyway.

"How long?"

"The doctor says in the next hour Molly should deliver. Everything's going like clockwork. Cam's so wonderful with her, Wes. He loves Molly so much...so much...."

He heard the anguish in Maggie's voice and drew her next to him. "Love does that to you," he agreed. "One of the many benefits."

"I—I never realized a man could be so tender...." Maggie made a frustrated sound. "That sounds stupid. You've been that way with me. Men have hearts that feel just as women do. Don't listen to my mutterings."

Wes smiled and caressed her tense back. The crimson cascade of hair around her head and shoulders gleamed beneath the kitchen lights. "It's been a highly emotional time for you, Maggie."

"For all of us."

Wes leaned down and pressed a kiss to her hair. Maggie made a muffled sound and turned, pressing herself against him. Surprised but pleased by her spontaneous gesture, he wrapped his arms around her. The words *I love you* begged to be torn from him and whispered into her ear, only inches from his mouth.

"It's hard to tell who's more excited by Molly's pregnancy." Wes chuckled, inhaling Maggie's clean, wholesome scent. "The Turk's out there talking about fatherhood. Dana's shaking her head no, but you can see a different answer in her eyes."

"I'll bet Dana will be a mother before long." Maggie laughed, absorbing Wes's strength and the gentleness he always shared with her.

"No bet. I think you're right. She'll handle it. Dana's good at straddling career and family demands."

Closing her eyes, Maggie sighed raggedly. Fear sat alongside her happiness at being in Wes's embrace.

Dana appeared at the entrance to the kitchen. "Maggie! It's time! Rachel's coming!"

Wes smiled and released Maggie so she could go help Molly. He ambled into the living room. Griff was standing, his hands in the pockets of his slacks. He'd taken off his dark blue jacket long ago, and the black tie, too. The collar of his white shirt was open.

Glancing at his watch, Wes saw it was midnight. Griff smiled over at him.

"Looks like that little girl's ready for 'launch' mode."

Wes chuckled and stood nearby, his hands on his hips. "Her first Cat shot into life," he agreed huskily. The look in Maggie's green eyes was something he wanted to imprint on the memory of his heart forever. She might pooh-pooh motherhood, marriage and children, but unconsciously, she appeared to be just as thrilled as if *she* were having the baby! Pursing his lips, Wes decided that no matter what time they left tonight after Rachel's birth, he was going to have a long, serious talk with Maggie. Time wasn't their friend anymore. It was their enemy. And he loved her.

Maggie sat down beside Molly on the bed and gripped her hand. Dana was on the other side. The doctor, midwife and Cam waited tensely as Rachel crowned and moved quickly down the birth canal. Molly's hair was wringing wet with sweat, and Maggie bathed her brow with a damp cloth.

"She's coming," Ruth Culver announced and smiled up at Molly.

Maggie was touched when both the doctor and midwife moved aside so that Cam, dressed in a white surgical gown and gloves, could catch his daughter as she emerged. Her breath suspended, Maggie heard Molly groan and give one last push. Her hand automatically tightened around Molly's.

Cam's face lit up with such awe as his baby daughter slipped into his waiting hands that Maggie felt tears rush to her eyes. The doctor spoke quietly to Cam and told him what to do. The midwife smiled.

"You have a lovely blond-haired little girl, Molly! Congratulations! She looks so much like you!"

Cam managed a short laugh of joy. He stared down at his daughter, so tiny in his hands. "Look at her," he whispered, his voice cracking. "Look at her...." He gently eased the baby up just enough so that Molly could get her first look at her daughter.

"Oh, Cam, she's so beautiful." Molly held out her hands to receive her daughter from him. Tears ran down Molly's cheeks as Cam brought their daughter over and laid her on her belly. Maggie moved so that Cam could sit beside his wife, with one hand on her and the other on his daughter. Backing away, Maggie watched as Cam tenderly leaned over, kissing Molly for a long, long time—a kiss sealing their love for each other; a love that was reflected in the baby who lay quietly, sheltered by their protective hands.

Sniffing, Maggie smiled. Dana's eyes were wet with tears. So were the midwife's and doctor's. There wasn't a dry eye in the place. Locating a box of tissues, Maggie passed them around.

"Maggie, will you tell Griff and Wes that Rachel's here?" Molly whispered, exhausted.

"You bet I will," she choked out. "I'll be back in a minute."

Wes looked up when the door to the bedroom opened. Maggie's eyes were bright with tears. He grew worried and took a step forward.

"Everything's fine," Maggie told both of them, seeing the sudden concern in Wes's eyes. "Rachel's here, and she's beautiful, just like her mother." Laughing shyly, Maggie blotted the tears from her eyes. "And everyone in there is crying. It's wonderful...."

In that instant, Wes knew he loved Maggie with a fierceness that would haunt him for the rest of his life. He gazed at her, savoring the softness and vulnerability that the birth had reflected in her. "That's great. Tell them all congratulations."

"Yeah," Griff whispered, managing a shy smile. "Tell the parents congratulations."

Maggie nodded and slipped back into the room. Already, Molly was sitting up in bed with pillows behind her back, nursing Rachel for the first time. Cam sat next to his wife, simply holding her hand and watching the baby reverently.

Maggie helped the midwife clear the room of unessential items, then turned out the overhead light, letting the lamp on the dresser shed its soft luminescence. She saw how exhausted Molly appeared.

"Why don't we leave her alone to get some sleep?" Maggie suggested to the group.

"Good idea," Ruth agreed. "My job's done, anyway. Time for me to go home and get some sleep."

Maggie watched everyone leave after hugging Molly, kissing the baby and congratulating Cam. Now they would be alone to share this special moment, and that's what Maggie had wanted. At the door, she heard Molly call her name.

"What?" Maggie asked softly, hesitating at the door.

"Do me one more favor before you leave?" Molly asked.

Maggie smiled. "Sure."

Molly gazed at Cam. "Will you take Rachel out and show her to Griff and Wes? I know they want to see her. It's not fair that they don't. They've been waiting, too."

Hesitating, Maggie felt heat surge up through her neck and cheeks. "Well... I'm not much at mothering, Molly, and—"

Cam laughed softly and picked up his daughter, now wrapped in a soft pink cotton blanket. "You're a woman, Maggie. This stuff comes naturally to you. It's us klutzy men who have to be trained."

When Cam placed Rachel in her arms, Maggie felt tears surge into her eyes. The baby had fine blond hair sprinkled all over her head. Her tiny bow-shaped lips were parted in sleep, and equally tiny hands curved together near her chin.

"I—thanks," she whispered. "She's so sweet, Molly. I'll be really careful with her. I won't be long."

"Maggie, she's not a carton of eggs. You don't need to stand there with that terrified look on your face," Molly said gently. "Just flow with your instincts. They're there, believe me."

It was like switching from one mode to another, or so Maggie thought as she gently carried Rachel out to the living room. Dana was standing in Griff's arms when she appeared. Wes was sitting on the couch, his face mirroring weariness coupled with happiness.

Maggie almost felt like the proud mother herself as Griff crowed over Rachel and delicately touched one of her perfectly formed hands. When she took the baby over for Wes to see, she grew all shaky inside, and even more emotional.

Wes placed his arm around Maggie, touched by the softness of her features as she held Rachel so carefully in her arms. He leaned over, lightly brushing the baby's still-damp hair and watched as she curled her fingers around his one large index finger.

"What a grip," he teased. "I wonder if she's going to be a jet jock, too."

Everyone laughed except Maggie. All she could do was absorb the child, marveling at her perfection. When she felt Wes lean over and kiss her on the cheek, she looked up, startled. What she saw in his shadowed eyes made her want to cry. The love in them stripped away the last barriers of her fear.

"Tell Molly and Cam that they have the most beautiful baby I've ever seen. And thank them for letting us be here, to take part in Rachel's birth."

Maggie nodded, aware of the reservoir of emotion in Wes's quiet voice. "I will. I'll be back in a minute."

Wes waited, resting his hands on his hips. Dana and Griff were leaving, going home, he was sure, to lie in each other's arms and welcome each other home. He told them good-night. Then, left alone in the living room, he pursed his mouth, picked up Maggie's bag and continued to wait. It was now or never. God knew, they were both shaken and highly emotional from sharing in the birth, but there was no more time left. Wes would talk to Maggie tonight.

Chapter Thirteen

Wes waited until they got inside Maggie's apartment before he said anything. The strain between them was palpable in the car, and it took everything he had to remain silent. A car was no place for this kind of discussion. It was one-thirty in the morning, and they were both depleted by the day's events.

Maggie nervously shut the door. "Do you—"

"I need to say—"

"I'm sorry, I interrupted. Would you like a glass of wine or something, before we go to bed?" Maggie asked, her breathing becoming erratic and panicky.

Wes smiled and shook his head. "We're running all over each other."

She stood uncertainly in the living room. Wes looked crisp and fresh in his chino slacks and lightweight crewneck sweater that reminded her of the color of champagne. "What?"

Wes approached her, his heart slamming hard into his ribs. He reached out, taking her hands. "Your fingers are ice cold," he murmured.

"Uh, yeah. They always get that way when I'm really nervous."

He smiled down at her. How young and pretty she looked with that mass of red hair curling lazily around her face and shoulders. "What are you nervous about?"

"Er, me . . . I mean, us. Well, sort of . . ."

"What about 'us'?" He saw the terrible fear in Maggie's huge green eyes and felt her stiffen.

Maggie's mouth grew very dry. She longed for a drink of water. "I . . . uh, God, this is hard, Wes. I'm so afraid."

Gently he smoothed her fiery red cheek with his fingertips. "So am I, Red. Come on, let's sit down and talk. Okay?"

She swallowed spasmodically. "Okay." It came out like a frog's croak. Maggie followed him to the couch and sat down. Wes never let go of her hands. She placed one leg beneath her and faced him. The silence deepened.

"Wes, I—"

"Maggie, I—"

"I'm sorry. Go ahead."

"No. You first, Red."

"I interrupted again. God, that's such a terrible habit."

"You've got more good habits than bad ones."

"I do?"

"I think so."

Nervously she pulled her hand from his and wiped her damp brow. "Wes, I've just got to say this before it eats me alive," Maggie blurted. "Ever since I met you, I've started to change. I didn't realize it at first, but Molly and Dana pointed it out to me. And then, after the first month, *you* did, too." Maggie shut her eyes. "Oh, God, I'm blithering like an idiot. An idiot!"

Wes laughed softly and framed her face with his hands. "Go on, Maggie. What you're saying is important to me. And you're not blithering. I'm following you."

"Oh, good." Maggie took a deep breath and tried to calm down. Touching the region of her heart, she blurted again, "I can feel my heart beating like a freight train in there. Can you hear it? You must, it's so loud."

Wes ached to take away the terrible fear in Maggie's eyes and voice. He wanted to kiss away her nervousness, but he knew Maggie had to do this in her own way. It was important she broach the fear barrier by herself. "I like what I see in your eyes, honey."

His words soothed Maggie to a degree. Closing her eyes, she muttered, "No one would believe I was a combat pilot, the way I'm acting now. Molly would call me a twit or something...." She forced herself to hold Wes's serious gaze. "Molly had a long talk with me two months ago. I came into her office all upset. I didn't know what to do with myself. I wasn't sleeping at night. I was more restless than I've ever been, day and night! I couldn't think two thoughts without thinking of you. If I closed my eyes, I saw your face. And when I finally did get to sleep, I'd dream of you.'' Maggie groaned and covered her face with her hand. ''This is embarrassing, Wes. Not only am I behaving like an immature teenager, I'm scared to death of how you'll react to what I've said.''

She bit down hard on her lower lip, looked away into the silent apartment and then looked back at him. ''I love you, Wes.'' There. It was out. Finally! Maggie sat unmoving, her eyes fixed on his for some indication of his reaction. ''I mean, I know it's crazy. I certainly didn't expect to fall in love with you. Your career after you leave the Navy is all mapped out. It's a sound plan. All these months, you've never said you loved me, and that's why it's so scary telling you how I really feel. I figured all along it was one-sided, but I had to get this off my chest before it killed me.

''And God knows, you may not feel a thing for me. I know we're great in bed together—good sex and all— but for me it's so much more than that. You make me happy. You've taught me so much about myself and the world around me.'' Maggie stopped abruptly. Then words she dredged out of herself came slowly and were filled with pain.

''I know you have to leave in two days. I'm trying to accept that, but I just don't seem to be able to. All through Red Flag, I wanted to cry because I was going to lose you.'' She wiped her eyes. ''And I didn't want to. Isn't that selfish and stupid of me? I'm in love with you. I don't even know if you love me, and yet—''

"Maggie," Wes whispered hoarsely, capturing her face between his hands, "I love the hell out of you. I love you just as much as you love me."

She sat there, stunned, looking into his blue eyes, smoldering with such promise that it made her cry that much more. Hunting around for a tissue and finding none, Maggie used the tail of her blouse to wipe her eyes.

"You do?"

"Yes."

"I—I didn't know. I was hoping—God, how I was hoping you loved me, Wes. Even if it was a little bit."

Gently he brought Maggie into his arms until she fitted against him on the couch, snug and protected. "I was afraid to tell you," Wes admitted against her hair.

"Why?" Maggie asked, holding him just as tightly, her heart soaring with such joy that she couldn't catch her breath.

With a sigh, he kissed her hair. "We'd gone through so much together in such a short, intense period of time, Maggie, that I wasn't sure if the situation forced us together out of survival, or if we really did fall in love regardless of what happened around us. I couldn't call it. I didn't know. You never lost your focus on Red Flag, even after the crash."

"But," Maggie whispered, looking up at his grim features, "I went to bed with you after the crash. We loved each other, Wes."

"I know. But a lot of guys go to bed with a woman and it means nothing. Or next to nothing," he muttered.

Indignant, Maggie retorted, "Well, I don't make a practice of going to bed with every guy I meet, Wes Bishop! Going to bed with you was a very serious commitment on my part."

"Now, don't get your temper up. I missed your silent message to me, Maggie. I'm sorry. That's why I never admitted that I loved you. You never *said* it to me, so I figured it was a one-way street from my end. It looks like we both read each other wrong."

She laid her head back against him. "You don't need to apologize. I guess I did the same thing to you. But you know how single jet jocks bed-hop sometimes."

"My commitment to you was just as strong, Red. I haven't been with a woman since my divorce from Jenny."

Touched, Maggie said nothing. In her heart of hearts, she knew Wes was loyal in a way few men ever would be—the same kind of loyalty her father had toward her mother. "I'm the one who should apologize," she whispered. "All those stereotypes really blinded me about you . . . us."

With a chuckle, Wes forced Maggie to sit up. Her eyes were lustrous with such love that he leaned over and pressed his mouth on hers. Heat and sweetness built between them, and Wes groaned at her response. In seconds, he deepened the exploratory kiss. If he didn't stop, he was going to pick Maggie up, carry her into the bedroom and make passionate love with her.

Loving her had to wait—at least, for a little while. Easing his mouth from her full lips, he drowned in her emerald gaze touched with molten-gold desire. "I love you, Maggie Donovan. With my life. For the rest of my life," Wes rasped thickly, tightening his hold on her shoulders. "I've got three months at sea. When I come home, I want to marry you. I want you for my wife. Will you marry me, then?"

The words fell softly around Maggie. The fierce fire of love burning in Wes's eyes told her everything. How blind could she have been, not to realize he honestly did love her? Parting her lips, she whispered, "Yes..."

A tremor of relief rippled through Wes. He shut his eyes. "Thank God," he murmured. Focusing his gaze back on Maggie, he frowned. "It's not going to be easy for us. You know that, don't you?"

Maggie nodded and placed her hands against his powerful chest. "Three months is an eternity."

"Pure hell."

"And after that? You said you had to go to flight school to qualify for the jumbo jets that UPS wanted you to fly."

Wes saw the loneliness in her eyes. "First things first. I want to marry you, Maggie. I want you to take your mandatory thirty days' leave when I get home."

"And then we'll go home—my home—to get married," Maggie began excitedly. "Mom has been wanting one of us girls to get married. She'd be heartbroken if we got married anywhere but in Sacramento."

Wes grinned. "That's fine. My parents will be happy to fly down and be there for the wedding."

"And after that?" The UPS school was on the East Coast and that meant they'd be separated again.

"I have some options, honey."

"What options? Why didn't you tell me this before? Here I'm thinking you'll be clear across the country and we'll be separated again for God knows how long!"

"Easy, my red-haired witch. Calm down." Wes laughed deeply, pulling Maggie back into his arms. "UPS wants to hire me as a pilot, no matter what kind of plane I fly. They need jumbo-jet-qualified pilots, but I could take on something smaller, so I'd be closer." He glanced down at her. "You know UPS flies out of Lindbergh Field down in San Diego, didn't you?"

"No."

"I could hire in, use San Diego as my base of operation for as long as you're stationed here. And then, when the Navy wants to move you to the next air station, I'll follow you. UPS is worldwide, and they fly into the remotest of countries, so we won't have to be separated again." Wes grinned triumphantly. "How's that sound to you? Think it's something you could live with?"

Maggie sighed audibly. "You know it is, you arrogant jet jock!"

"Good," Wes said, genuinely relieved. "Who knows? Maybe after your six-year enlistment's up, you might want to leave the Navy and fly as my copilot with UPS."

She snorted and sat up. "*Your* copilot? Give me a break, Bishop! I'll have enough flight hours by then to be pilot of my *own* plane!"

"I like it when you get indignant, do you know that? Your eyes get so huge and green. And that gold in them turns topaz with frustration." Wes watched her smile appear like sunlight after a storm. "Look, we've got four years on your enlistment to go. A lot of things could happen between now and then."

"What if I want to stay in the Navy and be a thirty-year woman?" Maggie challenged.

"Fine by me."

Sobering, Maggie held his dancing blue gaze. "What about children?"

"What about them?"

"I suppose you want a family right away like Cam and Molly have."

He threaded his fingers through her thick, silky hair. "Honey, my first priority is having you happy at whatever you want to do. I have a beautiful daughter I think the world of, and I'll always have her. Even though Annie lives with Jenny, we'll visit her from time to time. Eventually, once we get settled, I'd like to work something out with Jenny so that Annie can come and stay with us on certain holidays. I know she'll approve." He tousled her hair. "That way you can see if you like playing mom."

"And if I don't?"

"Maggie, I love you. I want to marry you because I happen to like you and think we can have a pretty good life together. Whether we have children or not is a mutual decision. If we don't have any, I'm not going to walk away from you."

She nodded. "I'm looking forward to meeting Annie, and I don't mind her staying with us."

"I knew you wouldn't," he teased her gently. "Just the way you were behaving with Rachel in your arms told me everything."

"Everything? What 'everything'?"

"You're getting upset again, Maggie."

"Well, what did you see? What do you know that I don't?"

Laughing again, Wes shook his head. He got up from the couch and held out his hand to her. "Come on, let's get a nice long, hot shower together and go to bed. One of these days, I'll tell you."

Maggie gazed up at his tall figure. Having children had never entered Maggie's mind, but now it did. "You're such a smart aleck when you want to be, Bishop," she accused, getting to her feet. Tossing her head, Maggie added, "And you don't know *everything!*"

Wes chuckled as Maggie marched by him, her shoulders thrown back, her chin at a proud angle. "Possibly," he murmured, following her down the hall toward the bedroom. His gut instinct told him that if Maggie did stay in the Navy, the day they assigned her to fly a desk instead of an airplane, she'd look for new goals to conquer. It was at that time, he surmised, that she just might look with favor upon becoming a mother.

Wes ambled down the hall, his hands in the pockets of his slacks. With or without children, Maggie was his world. Wes had never dreamed life would be given back to him in such a vivid, dramatic way as Maggie Donovan walking into his world and turning it upside down with her passion for living to the fullest. It was all he would ever need. What they had was a rare kind of love. He already knew that. Over time, Maggie would recognize it, too. Yes, they had an exciting life ahead of them. And he could hardly wait to share it with her. Forever.

* * * * *

Bestselling author **NORA ROBERTS** captures all the romance, adventure, passion and excitement of Silhouette in a special miniseries.

THE CALHOUN WOMEN

Four charming, beautiful and fiercely independent sisters set out on a search for a missing family heirloom—an emerald necklace—and each finds something even more precious...passionate romance.

Look for THE CALHOUN WOMEN miniseries starting in June.

COURTING CATHERINE
in Silhouette Romance #801 (June/$2.50)

A MAN FOR AMANDA
in Silhouette Desire #649 (July/$2.75)

FOR THE LOVE OF LILAH
in Silhouette Special Edition #685 (August/$3.25)

SUZANNA'S SURRENDER
in Silhouette Intimate Moments #397 (September/$3.25)

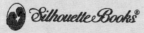 *Silhouette Books*®

Silhouette Special Edition

presents

SONNY'S GIRLS

by Emilie Richards, Celeste Hamilton and Erica Spindler

They had been Sonny's girls, irresistibly drawn to the charismatic high school football hero. Ten years later, none could forget the night that changed their lives forever.

In July—
ALL THOSE YEARS AGO by Emilie Richards (SSE #684)
Meredith Robbins had left town in shame. Could she ever banish the past and reach for love again?

In August—
DON'T LOOK BACK by Celeste Hamilton (SSE #690)
Cyndi Saint was Sonny's steady. Ten years later, she remembered only his hurtful parting words....

In September—
LONGER THAN . . . by Erica Spindler (SSE #696)
Bubbly Jennifer Joyce was everybody's friend. But nobody knew the secret longings she felt for bad boy Ryder Hayes....

SSESG-1

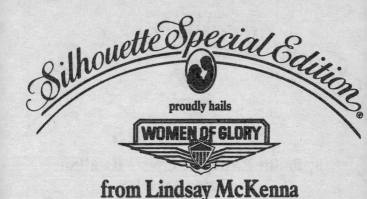

Silhouette Special Edition

proudly hails

WOMEN OF GLORY

from Lindsay McKenna

Soar with Dana Coulter, Molly Rutledge and Maggie Donovan—
Lindsay McKenna's WOMEN OF GLORY. On land, sea or air, these
three Annapolis grads challenge danger head-on, risking life and limb
for the glory of their country—and for the men they love!

May: NO QUARTER GIVEN (SE #667) Dana Coulter is on the brink
of achieving her lifelong dream of flying—and of meeting the man who
would love to take her to new heights!

June: THE GAUNTLET (SE #673) Molly Rutledge is determined
to excel on her own merit, but Captain Cameron Sinclair is equally
determined to take gentle Molly under his wing....

July: UNDER FIRE (SE #679) Indomitable Maggie never thought
her career—or her heart—would come under fire. But all that changes
when she teams up with Lieutenant Wes Bishop!

MILLION DOLLAR JACKPOT
SWEEPSTAKES RULES & REGULATIONS
NO PURCHASE NECESSARY TO ENTER OR RECEIVE A PRIZE

1. Alternate means of entry: Print your name and address on a 3" ×5" piece of plain paper and send to the appropriate address below.

In the U.S.	In Canada
MILLION DOLLAR JACKPOT	MILLION DOLLAR JACKPOT
P.O. Box 1867	P.O. Box 609
3010 Walden Avenue	Fort Erie, Ontario
Buffalo, NY 14269-1867	L2A 5X3

2. To enter the Sweepstakes and join the Reader Service, affix the Four Free Books and Free Gifts sticker along with both of your other Sweepstakes stickers to the Sweepstakes Entry Form. If you do not wish to take advantage of our Reader Service, but wish to enter the Sweepstakes only, do not affix the Four Free Books and Free Gifts sticker; affix only the Sweepstakes stickers to the Sweepstakes Entry Form. Incomplete and/or inaccurate entries are ineligible for that section or sections of prizes. Torstar Corp. and its affiliates are not responsible for mutilated or unreadable entries or inadvertent printing errors. Mechanically reproduced entries are null and void.

3. Whether you take advantage of this offer or not, on or about April 30, 1992, at the offices of D.L. Blair, Inc., Blair, NE, your sweepstakes numbers will be compared against the list of winning numbers generated at random by the computer. However, prizes will only be awarded to individuals who have entered the Sweepstakes. In the event that all prizes are not claimed, a random drawing will be held from all qualified entries received from March 30, 1990 to March 31, 1992, to award all unclaimed prizes. All cash prizes (Grand to Sixth) will be mailed to winners and are payable by check in U.S. funds. Seventh prize will be shipped to winners via third-class mail. These prizes are in addition to any free, surprise or mystery gifts that might be offered. Versions of this Sweepstakes with different prizes of approximate equal value may appear at retail outlets or in other mailings by Torstar Corp. and its affiliates.

4. PRIZES: (1) *Grand Prize $1,000,000.00 Annuity; (1) First Prize $25,000.00; (1) Second Prize $10,000.00; (5) Third Prize $5,000.00; (10) Fourth Prize $1,000.00; (100) Fifth Prize $250.00; (2,500) Sixth Prize $10.00; (6,000) **Seventh Prize $12.95 ARV.

   *This presentation offers a Grand Prize of a $1,000,000.00 annuity. Winner will receive $33,333.33 a year for 30 years without interest totalling $1,000,000.00.

   **Seventh Prize: A fully illustrated hardcover book, published by Torstar Corp. Approximate Retail Value of the book is $12.95.

   Entrants may cancel the Reader Service at any time without cost or obligation (see details in Center Insert Card).

5. Extra Bonus! This presentation offers an Extra Bonus Prize valued at $33,000.00 to be awarded in a random drawing from all qualified entries received by March 31, 1992. No purchase necessary to enter or receive a prize. To qualify, see instructions in Center Insert Card. Winner will have the choice of any of the merchandise offered or a $33,000.00 check payable in U.S. funds. All other published rules and regulations apply.

6. This Sweepstakes is being conducted under the supervision of D.L. Blair, Inc. By entering the Sweepstakes, each entrant accepts and agrees to be bound by these rules and the decisions of the judges, which shall be final and binding. Odds of winning the random drawing are dependent upon the number of entries received. Taxes, if any, are the sole responsibility of the winners. Prizes are nontransferable. All entries must be received at the address on the detachable Business Reply Card and must be postmarked no later than 12:00 MIDNIGHT on March 31, 1992. The drawing for all unclaimed Sweepstakes prizes and for the Extra Bonus Prize will take place on May 30, 1992, at 12:00 NOON at the offices of D.L. Blair, Inc., Blair, NE.

7. This offer is open to residents of the U.S., United Kingdom, France and Canada, 18 years or older, except employees and immediate family members of Torstar Corp., its affiliates, subsidiaries and all other agencies, entities and persons connected with the use, marketing or conduct of this Sweepstakes. All Federal, State, Provincial, Municipal and local laws apply. Void wherever prohibited or restricted by law. Any litigation within the Province of Quebec respecting the conduct and awarding of a prize in this publicity contest must be submitted to the Régie des Loteries et Courses du Québec.

8. Winners will be notified by mail and may be required to execute an affidavit of eligibility and release, which must be returned within 14 days after notification or an alternate winner may be selected. Canadian winners will be required to correctly answer an arithmetical, skill-testing question administered by mail, which must be returned within a limited time. Winners consent to the use of their name, photograph and/or likeness for advertising and publicity in conjunction with this and similar promotions without additional compensation.

9. For a list of our major prize winners, send a stamped, self-addressed envelope to: MILLION DOLLAR WINNERS LIST, P.O. Box 4510, Blair, NE 68009. Winners Lists will be supplied after the May 30, 1992 drawing date.

Offer limited to one per household.

LTY-S791